PROTECTING OUR WORLD

Contents

Series consultant: David Duthie

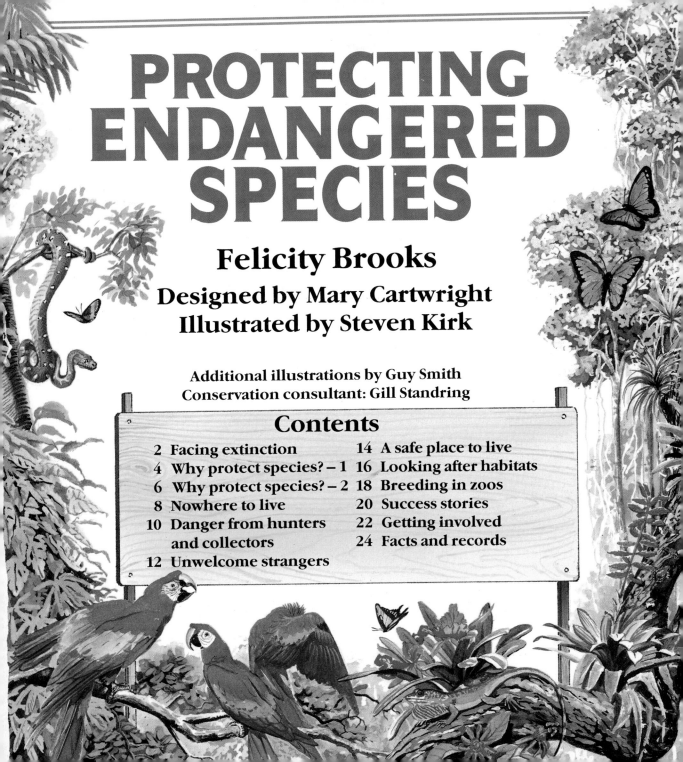

PROTECTING ENDANGERED SPECIES

Felicity Brooks

Designed by Mary Cartwright
Illustrated by Steven Kirk

Additional illustrations by Guy Smith
Conservation consultant: Gill Standring

Contents

Facing extinction

Nearly all of the millions of different types of plants and animals that have ever lived on Earth have died out, or become extinct. New plants and animals develop to replace older ones. This happens very slowly over millions of years, and is called evolution. Many species lived and died before the first people appeared.

Tyrannosaurus rex was about 12m (13yds) long.

Dinosaurs lived on Earth for 100 million years. They became extinct 65 million years ago.

Species

A species is a group of animals or plants which is different from all other groups. Members of the group can breed together.

There are 300 different species of hummingbirds, 20,000 species of butterflies and about 25,000 species of orchids.

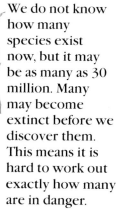

We do not know how many species exist now, but it may be as many as 30 million. Many may become extinct before we discover them. This means it is hard to work out exactly how many are in danger.

Becoming extinct

When the very last animal or plant of a species dies, that species is said to have become extinct. It cannot be brought back. It has gone forever.

Orange Band, the very last dusky seaside sparrow, died in 1989.

Natural causes

In the past, species became extinct because of natural causes. Some may have died out because of changes in the Earth's weather. Others died out when new species appeared which were better at finding food and better suited to the conditions.

Some of the species which lived on Earth 200 million years ago.

Some of the species 50 million years ago

Extinction facts

★Three-quarters of the extinctions which have happened in the last 300 years were caused by humans.

★We are likely to cause the extinction of a quarter of all known species in the next 20 years, unless we work to protect them.

★Species are becoming extinct 1,000 times faster than they did before humans appeared.

★We have already killed off 17 species of bears, four of cats and three of deer.

★By the time you finish reading this book, another species will be extinct.

Mysterious thylacines

Thylacines are marsupials – they carry their babies in a pouch. They are the size of large dogs. Over 4,000 were killed by hunters in Tasmania between 1888 and 1909.

Thylacines are also called Tasmanian tigers because of their stripes.

The last thylacine was thought to have died in Hobart Zoo in Tasmania in 1936.

AUSTRALIA

Tasmania

Recently people say they have seen thylacines in Tasmania. Some even say they have seen them in Australia. Experts thought they died out there thousands of years ago. No one knows if this species is extinct.

In danger

When there are very few of a species left, that species is in great danger of becoming extinct and it is called an endangered species.

The black rhinoceros is an endangered species. There were 15,000 in 1979. Now there are less than 3,000. The four other species of rhinos are also endangered. You can find out more about the problems rhinos face on page 10.

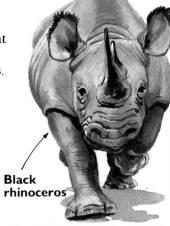

Black rhinoceros

Human causes

Now most species become extinct because of things humans do, such as cutting down the forests which animals live in. There are now over five billion humans but other species are disappearing fast.

WANTED

Human – the most dangerous species

How many in danger?

Some scientists think a million species are endangered and may become extinct by the year 2000, unless we act to protect them. These include:

25,000 species of plants

1,000 species of birds

over 500 species of mammals

Why protect species? – 1

We must try to stop so many species from becoming extinct. If just one species disappears, many others may suffer. This is because all species, including humans, rely on others to survive. Species are connected in many ways, as shown below.

Tree fact

★When one oak tree is cut down, it may affect as many as 280 other species. This is because they are all connected to the tree in some way in a food web.

Food webs

Each species needs others for food and may itself be eaten by others. Many species are connected in this way in a food web.

Food webs are delicately balanced and easily upset. If one species dies out, the whole web changes. Here is part of a food web in an oak wood.

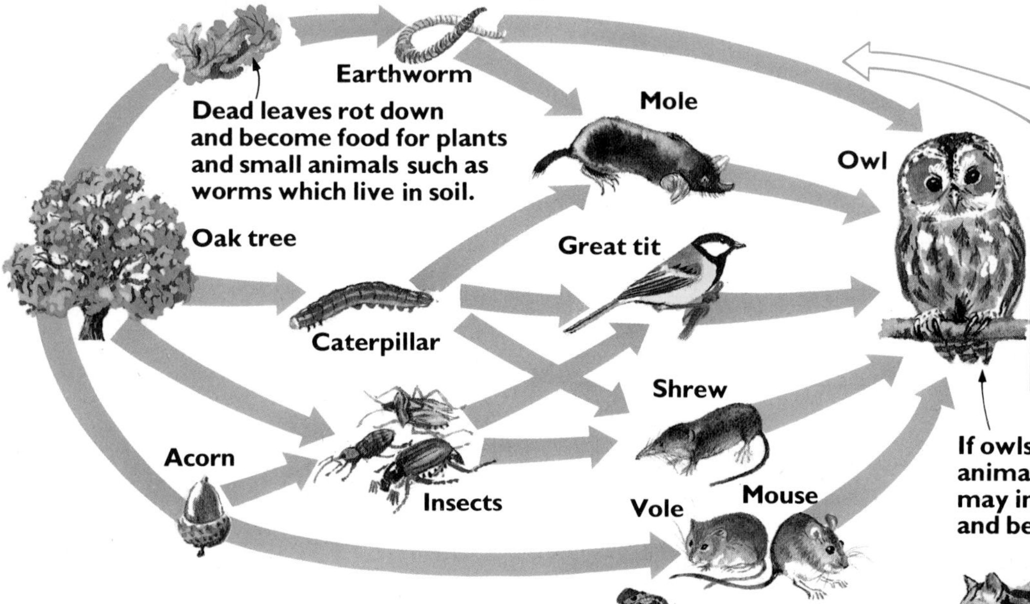
Earthworm
Dead leaves rot down and become food for plants and small animals such as worms which live in soil.
Mole
Owl
Oak tree
Great tit
Caterpillar
Shrew
Acorn
Insects
Vole
Mouse

An arrow from one species to another shows that the first species is eaten by the second. For example, insects are eaten by shrews and shrews are eaten by owls.

If owls become rare, the animals which they eat may increase in number and become pests.

Upsetting the balance

These are two examples of food webs which have been upset when species have become endangered.

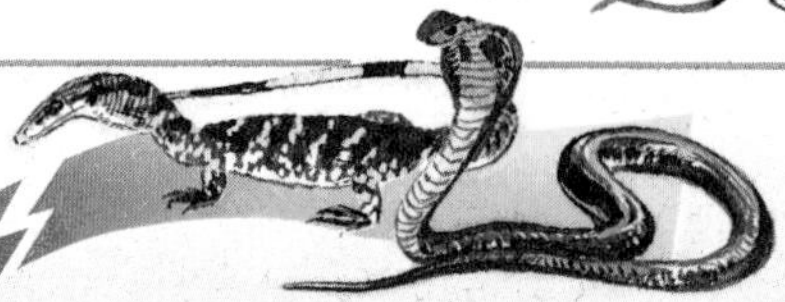

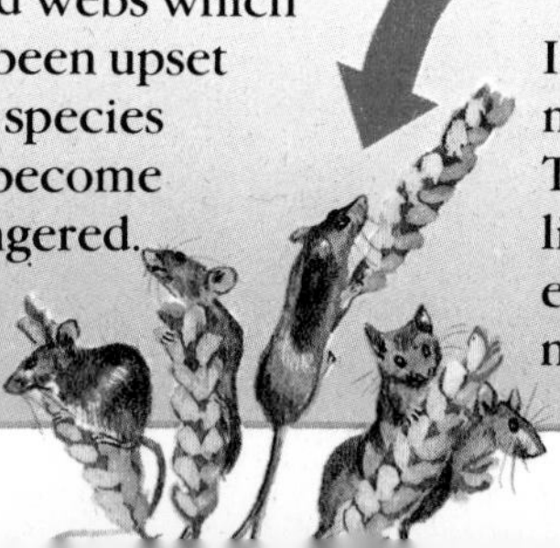

In India, people killed many lizards and snakes. The mice which the lizards and snakes used to eat have increased in number and eaten crops.

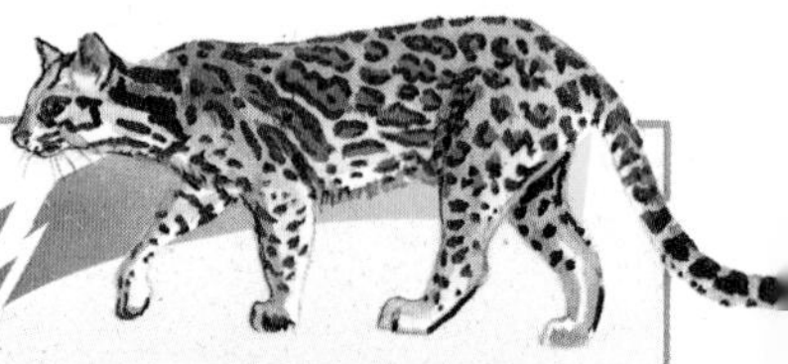

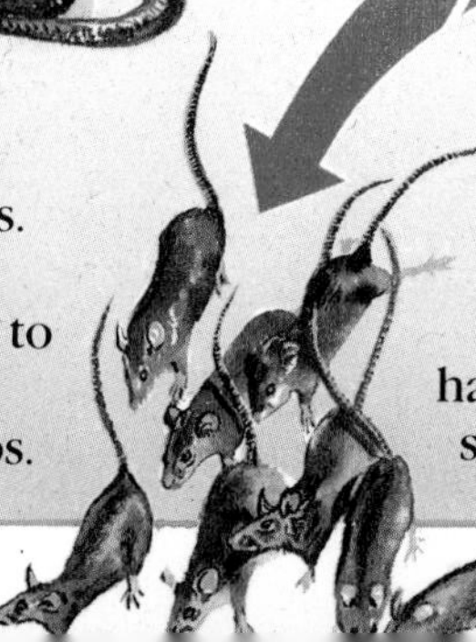

In South America and Africa, large wild cats, such as ocelots, are now very rare. The rats which they used to kill have grown in number and spread disease to humans.

Fruitful flying foxes

Species are connected in other ways. Many trees and animals, for example, depend on fruit bats. Fruit bats are also called flying foxes. Some species are already extinct and 200 more are endangered.

Carrying pollen

Some trees where the fruit bats live have flowers which only open at night. The bats fly from tree to tree, sipping nectar from their flowers.

Fruit bat sipping nectar

As they fly, the bats carry pollen between the trees. The flowers need this pollen to form seeds that can grow into new trees.

Spreading seeds

Fruit bats eat figs, dates, mangoes and other fruit.

The bats help spread seeds by eating fruit. The seeds in the fruit go through their bodies and pass out in droppings as the bats fly over the forest.

Some seeds grow into new trees in place of ones which have died.

If we allow fruit bats to be killed off, then the trees will also die out.

Others in danger

Monkeys, parrots, insects and other animals rely on the trees for food and shelter. They are in danger when the trees die out. People who eat the fruit and farmers who grow it to sell suffer too.

Bat facts

★Bats live in most parts of the world. There are over 1,000 species. Many are endangered.

★Nearly a quarter of all mammal species are bats.

★Fruit bats are killed for food and because some people believe they are pests.

★Since the beginning of 1990, all fruit bats have been protected by international law.

★Look at page 22 to find out how you can help protect bats.

Depending on dodos

Dodo

Dodos lived on the island of Mauritius. They became extinct over 300 years ago but this still has an effect today. Only a few old Calvaria trees are left on the island. Scientists believe the trees needed the dodos to eat their fruit, grind up the seeds and pass them out in droppings. The seeds cannot grow without this happening, so there are no new trees.

Calvaria tree

Why protect species? – 2

We depend on many species of animals and plants for food, medicines, clothes and other things. Many more species may also be useful. We need to find out about these because we shall need them in the future. This will not be possible if the species become extinct before they can be studied.

Plant potential

There are about 80,000 plants which can be eaten. At the moment most people in the world depend on about 20. Scientists are finding other food plants which may become important in the future.

There would be no chocolate today if cocoa trees had become extinct.

Bananas

Pineapple

Avocados

Oranges

Lemons

Brazil nuts

Rice

Tea

Coffee

All these foods first came from wild plants that grow in rain forests. Thousands of other forest plants can be eaten, but many are endangered as forests are being destroyed.

Food for the future

Scientists need to conserve as many different types of wild plants and animals as possible. They can cross-breed them with farm plants and animals to make new crops and food animals which are stronger and do not catch diseases.

Buffaloes

Wild buffaloes do not catch diseases and have good meat. They could be cross-bred with farm buffaloes to make strong, healthy food animals, but they are endangered in many areas.

Asiatic wild buffaloes are an endangered species.

Cross-breeding

Scientists can mate an animal or plant with one of a slightly different kind to make a new type of plant or animal. This is called cross-breeding.

Teosinte

Teosinte is a type of wild maize which can grow in cool, damp places. It gets very few diseases and does not have to be replanted every year.

The last Teosinte plants were found and saved by plant experts just before the forest where they grew was cleared.

Scientists are cross-breeding teosinte with other kinds of maize to make strong new crop plants.

Many people depend on maize for food. Growing new kinds will help make sure they have enough to eat.

Fuel from the forest

Many people now rely on coal, oil and gas for fuel. These may run out, so we must find new fuels. Fuels from trees and plants which do not run out may provide some of our needs in the future.

Babassu palm

Fuel facts

★A fuel made from sugar cane is used to run cars in Brazil.

★The fruit of petroleum nut trees produce an oil similar to petrol.

★The fruit of babassu palms contain oil which is used to make food, soap and many other things. The outside of the fruit (husk) can be burnt as fuel.

Marvellous medicines

Plants and animals can be used to make medicines. Half our medicines already come from plants. Many more species could be useful, though only a tiny number have been studied.

Coral may be a source of important new medicines but many types are endangered.

Poison from frogs in Central America is used as an ingredient in some new medicines.

A medicine made from rosy periwinkle plants now helps to cure children of leukemia (a type of cancer). This would not have been known if the plant had become extinct 20 years ago.

Variety

It is dangerous to depend on too few species for food. If a species is affected by disease many people may starve.

Farmers in Peru grow over 3,000 different types of potatoes. If one type is affected by disease they can eat others.

In the 1800s, European farmers only grew a few types of potato. In 1845 most of their crop was killed by a disease. Many people starved because they had no other food.

Enjoying our world

Plants and animals are useful, but also beautiful. We enjoy studying and looking at them. We feel very sad when a species becomes extinct.

Imagine a world without birds, butterflies or wild flowers. We must act quickly to protect all our species for the future.

Spider monkeys

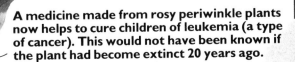

Nowhere to live

On the next six pages you can discover some of the reasons why animals and plants become endangered. The main danger comes from humans destroying or damaging species' living places, or habitats.

Habitats

Habitats provide species with all the things they need, such as food, water, shelter and a place to bring up young. Each species is suited to its own habitat and usually cannot live anywhere else.

Giant pandas live in bamboo forests in China and eat bamboo. Most of the forests where they used to live have been cleared for farmland.

Area where pandas lived in the past.

CHINA

Areas where they live today.

A special place

Within each habitat, every species has a special place (niche). In a rain forest, for example, some live in the tree tops, others on the ground.

Sloths live in the trees and sometimes go down to the ground.

Three-toed sloth

Size of habitats

Each species needs a certain amount of space. This may be huge or quite small. When part of a habitat is destroyed, too many animals crowd into an area where there may not be enough food and shelter for them all.

This species of moth lives its whole life in the fur of a sloth.

Every jaguar needs 250km² of land.

Harpy eagles live in the very tallest trees.

Parrots and monkeys live in the tree tops where they can find fruit and nuts to eat.

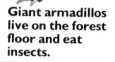

Giant armadillos live on the forest floor and eat insects.

Destroying habitats

When their habitats are destroyed or changed by humans, many species have little chance of survival. Even if they are not hunted, they will die out if they have nowhere to live. These are some of the ways humans destroy and harm habitats.

Cutting down forests

Forests are cut down to provide wood and land for fields, roads and buildings.

Rain forests are the home of millions of species, but nearly half the rain forests in the world have already been cut down. When the forests disappear, millions of animals and plants die.

Rafflesia flowers are the largest in the world. They can grow to nearly 1m (1yd) wide. They live only in rain forests in Indonesia.

21 species of lemurs on the island of Madagascar are endangered. They have lost three-quarters of their forest habitat in the last 50 years.

◀ Ring-tailed lemur

◀ The few mountain gorillas left in forests in Central Africa are endangered by loss of habitat.

Pollution

Pollution affects every part of the world and harms animals and their habitats. Most damage has been done in the past 50 years.

Fumes from cars and factories pollute the air.

Litter may harm habitats and can be dangerous.

Poisonous chemicals from factories and farms get into the water and soil.

Changing land use

As the human population grows, more and more habitats are destroyed. Hedges and woods are cut down to make fields, ponds and marshes are drained, roads are built on moors and houses are built on meadows.

Fish, birds and other water animals cannot live in polluted water. Pollution also kills plants.

Pesticides

Pesticides are poisonous chemicals used to kill insects. They build up in a food web (see page 4) when big animals eat smaller ones which have been poisoned.

Peregrine falcon

Many birds of prey, such as falcons and eagles began to die off when the pesticide DDT was used. DDT has now been banned in some areas and numbers are increasing again.

9

Danger from hunters and collectors

Wild animals are sometimes captured to be pets or hunted for valuable parts of their bodies. Many plants are dug up for people's collections.

When too many animals and plants are taken from the wild or killed, a species becomes endangered and then extinct.

The price of beauty

Beautiful animals such as big cats and snakes are killed for their skins. The skins are made into coats, bags and so on. Most of the killing is illegal. It still happens because people buy things made from these skins.

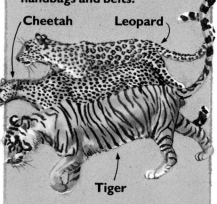

Black caiman

A million caimans are killed illegally every year. Their skins are made into wallets, shoes, handbags and belts.

Cheetah   **Leopard**

Tiger

Cheetahs, leopards and tigers are hunted for their striped or spotted skins.

Elephants

Until 1990, 100,000 African elephants ▶ were killed each year for their ivory tusks which were made into jewellery and other things. Most were killed by poachers (illegal hunters) who can make a lot of money by selling tusks.

Poachers prefer to kill males because of their large tusks. In some parts of Africa there are very few males left.

ELEPHANT ALARM

In 1979, there were 1.3 million African elephants. Now there are about 600,000. Most countries agreed to ban the buying and selling of ivory in 1990. This may be the last chance for the elephants.

When their mothers are killed, baby elephants cannot survive. Every time a female is shot, at least one baby dies.

Rhinos

Rhinoceroses are also in great danger ▶ of extinction. Poachers kill them for their horns. These are made into dagger handles and medicines in some parts of the world.

Killing rhinos is illegal but very hard to stop. One horn can be worth £50,000 ($85,000). In Namibia in Africa, people are trying to save the rhinos by sawing off their horns. This does not hurt the rhinos but may stop them being killed.

Saving the whales

Species of whales, such as humpbacks and blue whales, have been hunted almost to extinction for their meat, bones and oil. Most countries have now agreed to stop the killing but it will be a long time before whales are out of danger.

Blue whale

The danger of pets

Many species are endangered because too many animals have been taken from the wild to be sold as pets.

Parrots are taken from the ▶ wild and sold to pet shops. For each parrot that ends up in a shop, four more die on the journey. About 100 parrot species are in danger.

Rainbow lorikeet

Before 1981, millions of ▶ tortoises were taken from Africa to Europe to be sold as pets. Many died on the journey and very few lived longer than three years as pets (they should live to be 20). This trade has now stopped, but two species are rare because of it.

Collecting plants

People take plants from the wild to put in their gardens or collections. This is why many plants become endangered.

Golden barrel cacti are now very rare in Mexico because of illegal collection.

In Asia, 35 species of slipper orchids are in danger because so many have been taken from the wild.

How to help

★Do not buy souvenirs or other things made from parts of animals such as ivory, fur, snakeskin or coral.

★Never take plants from the wild or pick wild flowers.

★If you buy a pet, check that it was born in captivity and not taken from the wild.

★Look at pages 22 and 23 to find out more about how you can help stop hunting and collecting.

Hunted to extinction

In 1800, there were over three billion passenger pigeons in North America. During the next 100 years they were shot by hunters for sport and food. There were none left in the wild by 1900. The very last one died in Cincinnati Zoo in 1914.

One flock of passenger pigeons was over 500km (311 miles) long. It took 3 days to fly over a town.

Unwelcome strangers

When humans take plants and animals from one country to another and allow them to become wild, it can endanger the native species (species already living in a country).

The new arrivals may compete with native species for food and space and give them diseases. They may spread out of control and cause many problems.

The Galapagos Islands

The animals on the Galapagos Islands have developed separately from the rest of the world's species. They are not found anywhere else. They are in danger from newer arrivals such as cats, pigs and dogs. People brought these animals to the islands as pets or for food. They have become wild and bred fast.

Ecuador
SOUTH AMERICA
The Galapagos Islands are 965km (600mi) from Ecuador

◄ Some giant tortoises are over 100 years old and have shells one metre (over one yard) long. There used to be 15 species. Now there are 11. When 'Lonesome George', the very last of the Pinta Island tortoises, dies, there will only be 10.
— Land iguana

Most of Galapagos is now a protected area (see page 14). People are trying to find ways of controlling the unwelcome strangers but it is hard, as they breed so fast.

Dangerous invaders

These are some of the animals which endanger the wildlife of the Galapagos.

Herds of goats strip bark off trees and compete with tortoises and land iguanas for food.

Pigs eat young tortoises, tortoise eggs and birds' eggs. They kill plants by digging for roots.

Wild cats eat iguanas and baby tortoises.

Packs of dogs eat marine iguanas and penguins.

Black rats got on to the islands from ships. They eat seeds, flowers, young birds, tortoises and eggs.

Galapagos cormorants cannot fly, so are unable to escape from enemies.

Galapagos penguins are the only penguin species that lives on the equator. Most penguins live in cold climates.

Marine iguanas are the only lizards in the world that swim in the sea. They go out at low tide to eat seaweed.

Coypu chaos

In 1932, coypus from South America escaped from English fur farms into marshes in East Anglia. They increased in number and ate crops, rare plants and birds. They also damaged habitats such as river banks. It has taken over 50 years to get rid of them.

← Coypu

Fierce fish

In 1960, some fish called Nile perch were put into three lakes in Africa to provide food for local people. The perch have eaten so many other fish in the lakes that a third of the 1000 native species have become extinct.

The Nile perch were put into these 3 lakes.

Lake Victoria
Lake Tanganyika
Lake Malawi

Arrivals in Australia

Even on large islands, new arrivals can cause problems. These species have helped endanger some of Australia's unusual animals.

AUSTRALIA

Rabbit explosion

24 rabbits brought from England in 1859 bred fast until there were billions. They ate crops and harmed habitats.

Foxes brought to kill the rabbits ate native species as well. Finally a disease was introduced to control the rabbits, though even now they are pests.

Some species of wallabies are endangered because they have to compete with rabbits, sheep and goats for food.

Wallaby

Toad plague

In 1935, cane toads were brought to Australia from South America. Farmers hoped they would eat the beetles which were killing their sugar cane. The huge, poisonous toads spread fast. They are now a threat to native frogs, reptiles and small mammals.

Cane toad

Prickly problems

Prickly pear cacti were brought to Australia as garden plants in the 1800s. They spread in the wild to cover 27 million hectares (67 million acres) of land by 1925. The cacti are now under control. Insects were introduced to kill them.

World's worst weed

Water hyacinths from South America spread fast. They now cover huge areas of water in Asia, Australia and the USA. People introduce them because they look pretty, but they block up rivers and lakes and poison fish.

Killer worms

Flatworms from New Zealand came to Northern Ireland in the soil of potted plants. They have escaped into the wild and spread. They kill earthworms which are needed to keep soil healthy. So far, scientists have found no way to control them.

13

A safe place to live

On the following pages you can find out about some of the ways humans can protect endangered species. The best way is to set aside areas of land or water where animals and plants can live safely. These are called protected areas. They are places such as bird sanctuaries and national parks.

National parks

There are about 1,240 national parks around the world. The first national park was Yellowstone in the USA. It was set aside in 1872.

Yellowstone National Park covers a huge area of mountains and forests. It is about half the size of Wales. Moose, bison, elk, pumas, lynx, bears and many other animals live there.

Each grizzly bear needs a lot of space. Even in Yellowstone there is only room for 20 or 30 of them.

Serengeti National Park is in Tanzania, Africa. It is home to over two million large animals including rhinos, leopards, zebras, giraffes and wildebeest.

Wildebeest are a type of antelope. In the spring, huge herds of them cross the enormous Serengeti plain to find water.

Park problems
It can be difficult to set aside a national park without upsetting the people who live in the area. Also, many parks are short of money and do not have enough workers, vehicles and other things they need to protect their wildlife properly.

Operation Tiger

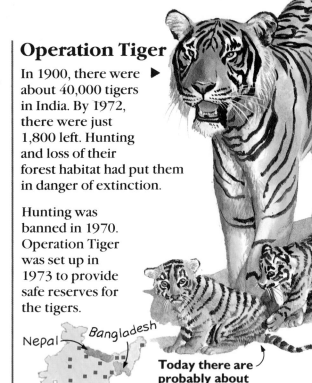

In 1900, there were ▶ about 40,000 tigers in India. By 1972, there were just 1,800 left. Hunting and loss of their forest habitat had put them in danger of extinction.

Hunting was banned in 1970. Operation Tiger was set up in 1973 to provide safe reserves for the tigers.

Nepal — Bangladesh

India

Today there are probably about 4,000 tigers in India.

The red squares show the Operation Tiger reserves.

On some reserves it is hard to protect the forests from people who need firewood and land for crops. Some tigers are still killed by poachers who sell their skins.

Water reserves

Water animals and plants also need a safe place to live. There are protected areas in the sea called marine reserves.

Manatees are rare water mammals. Each year many are killed or injured by the propellers of boats. Now they are being helped by reserves near the coast of Florida, USA.

Moving species

Sometimes species are moved from a habitat which is in danger to a safer place. Animals may be put to sleep for a short time while they are being moved.

Polar bears are moved away from towns to stop them being killed by frightened humans.

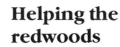

Wildlife gardens

Small protected areas can also help wildlife. Even a small garden can provide a habitat for many species.

Wildlife gardeners do not use chemical pesticides (see page 9) or anything else which might be harmful to wildlife.

Compost heap

Stinging nettles are food for caterpillars.

Wild flowers

Bird box

Long grass and weeds shelter insects.

Helping the redwoods

Plants as well as animals need protected habitats. Giant redwood trees, for example, are now only found in Northern California in a protected area.

Giant redwoods are the largest trees in the world. They can grow to over 80m (87yds) tall.

Manatee

Many insects and fungi live on rotting logs. Bushes shelter birds.

Ponds provide homes for frogs, toads, newts and other water animals and plants.

Buddleia bushes attract butterflies.

Honeysuckle plants attract insects.

Bird table to feed birds

Safe place facts

★Protected areas cover less than one twenty-fifth of the world's land surface.

★The largest protected area is in Greenland. It is bigger than Finland and Norway put together.

★Etosha National Park in Namibia, Africa is the largest national park. It is a third of the size of Italy. It was set aside in 1907.

★The Great Barrier Reef in Australia is the largest marine reserve. It is 2,027km (1,260 miles) long.

Looking after habitats

Most species in the world do not live in protected areas. It is important that we look after all natural habitats. We must find ways of farming, fishing and enjoying the countryside that do not damage the world we live in.

Farming with chemicals

A lot of land belongs to farmers. Some modern methods of farming, like those shown below, use many chemicals. These methods can produce a lot of food cheaply, but may harm wildlife.

There are few trees or hedges, so there is very little food and shelter for animals.

Farmers grow few kinds of crops and kill all weeds with chemicals. Not many species can live in this habitat.

Big fields are easy to look after with modern machines, but their soil is easily swept away by wind and rain.

Pesticides kill useful insects, such as bees, as well as pests. They may also poison other animals in a food web.

Chemical fertilizers may seep into rivers and poison the animals in them.

Farming for wildlife

Not all farmers use chemicals. In some places, such as parts of France, farmers use older methods. This kind of farming is much better for wildlife. Until about 30 years ago, many farms were like this.

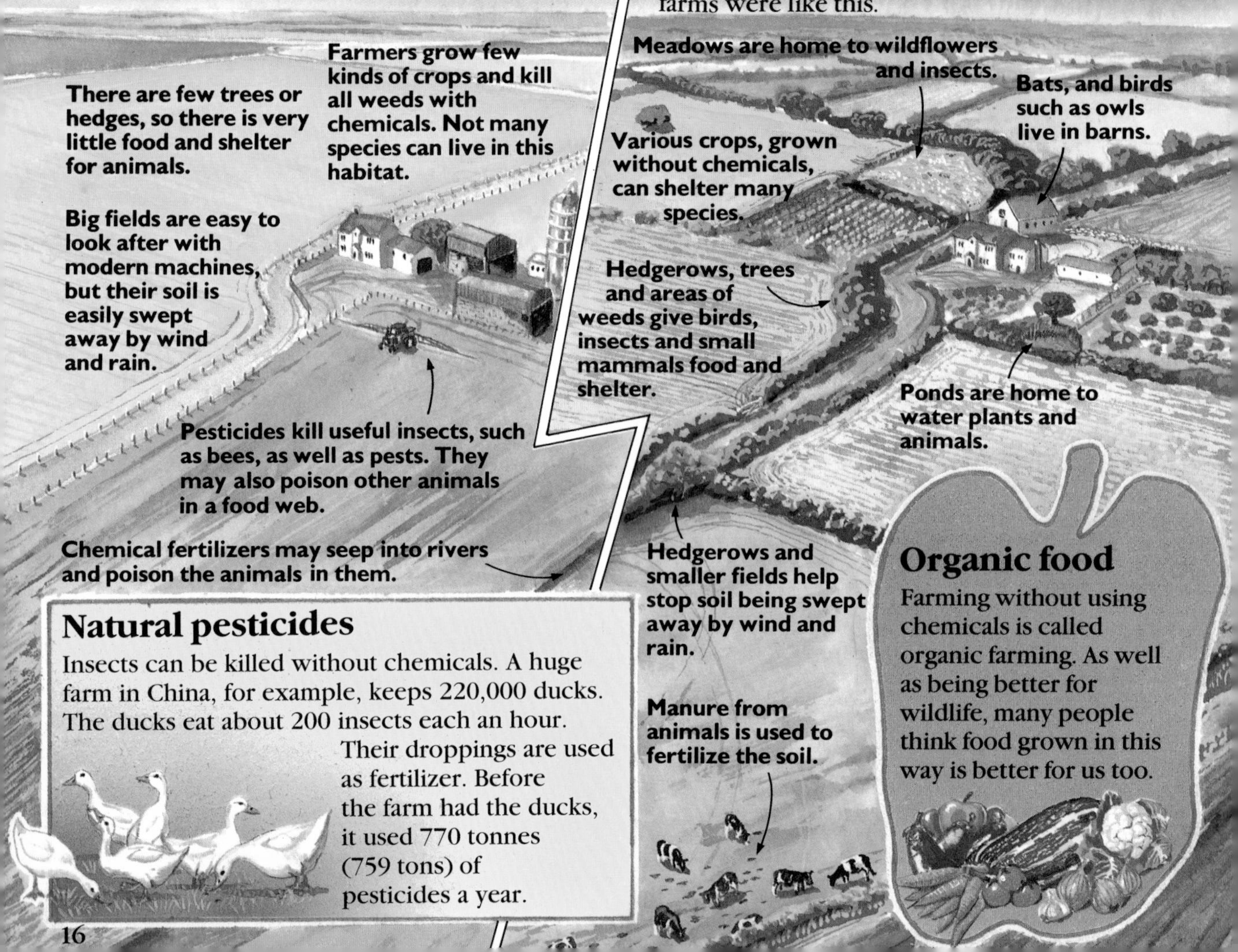

Meadows are home to wildflowers and insects.

Bats, and birds such as owls live in barns.

Various crops, grown without chemicals, can shelter many species.

Hedgerows, trees and areas of weeds give birds, insects and small mammals food and shelter.

Ponds are home to water plants and animals.

Hedgerows and smaller fields help stop soil being swept away by wind and rain.

Manure from animals is used to fertilize the soil.

Natural pesticides

Insects can be killed without chemicals. A huge farm in China, for example, keeps 220,000 ducks. The ducks eat about 200 insects each an hour. Their droppings are used as fertilizer. Before the farm had the ducks, it used 770 tonnes (759 tons) of pesticides a year.

Organic food

Farming without using chemicals is called organic farming. As well as being better for wildlife, many people think food grown in this way is better for us too.

Taking care of the countryside

People often harm habitats when they are out in the countryside. Follow these rules to help make sure you do not do any damage.

Keep to paths – do not tread on plants, dig them up or pick wild flowers.

Take all litter home with you.

Be careful not to start a fire. Fires kill millions of animals and plants every year.

Keep dogs under control.

Never throw things into the sea or into rivers, streams, ponds or lakes.

Do not damage trees, walls, hedges, paths or fences.

Close all gates behind you.

Do not disturb wild animals.

Fishing dangers

Thousands of mute swans and other water birds have been killed by swallowing lead weights which fishermen have left behind.

If you go fishing, use harmless non-toxic weights. Take all line, floats and hooks home. These also kill animals.

Poisoned swans cannot hold their necks upright.

Letting people know

When conservationists work to save species, they must let local people know what they are doing. People who understand what is going on can help to protect habitats, stop hunting and so on.

Conservationists are working to ▶ replant a forest in Guanacaste National Park in Costa Rica. They want to make the park into a 'living class room'. Local people visit the park to learn about the forest and help plant trees.

The tapir is one of the endangered animals that lives in the park.

◀ In the Philippines, people working to save monkey-eating eagles use films, leaflets and posters to get local people interested in the project.

Monkey-eating eagle

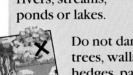

A van travels around schools and villages in ▶ Rwanda in Africa. It shows films and slides which explain why it is important to protect the gorillas that live there.

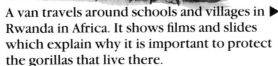

Breeding in zoos

Some animals endangered in the wild are taken to zoos where they may be helped to breed and increase in number. This is called captive breeding. Some may then be released back into the wild.

Captive breeding is only used as a last attempt to save species. At most, it could probably save 1000 of all the species in the world. Protecting habitats, stopping hunting and so on are much more successful.

Helping breeding

Scientists must find out a lot about a species to help it breed. They must know what it eats, how it likes to live, how to treat its illnesses and so on. Animals which are ill or unhappy will not breed.

Return of the bison

American bison were probably the first animals to be saved from extinction by captive breeding. In 1830 there were 60 million bison. By 1894, hunters had reduced their numbers to less than 100.

A few bison taken to the Bronx Zoo in New York and other places bred well. Many were later let back into new national parks.

Today there are about 90,000 American bison.

Golden lion tamarins

These little monkeys faced extinction when their forest homes in Brazil were cleared for farmland. Now they are being bred in zoos around the world. Over 50 a year are born in captivity and more than 70 have been let back into a protected area in Brazil. They are taught to move around and find food inside big cages in the forest before release.

Golden lion tamarins live in groups of 3 to 8. Each group needs 40 hectares (99 acres) of forest.

Operation Oryx

In 1962, three endangered Arabian oryx were rescued from the desert of Oman, just before hunters reached them. The oryx were taken to Phoenix Zoo, USA. Oryx from other zoos were brought there to make a world herd.

Arabian oryx

In 1972, the last wild oryx were shot, but those in zoos were breeding. A herd put back into a reserve in Oman in 1980 is doing well. It is guarded by a local tribe.

Back to the wild

Animals bred in zoos are not used to surviving in the wild. They have to learn to find food, avoid enemies and compete with other animals. They will not survive long if the conditions that made them endangered are still there.

Only 1 in 10 barn owls bred in captivity survives for more than 10 months in the wild.

Breeding successes

These are some other animals which have been helped by captive breeding.

In the USA, red wolves became extinct in the wild, but there were packs in 12 zoos. 39 wolves were released back into the wild in 1987. Now there are more than 100.

The number of snow leopards in zoos increased from 130 in 1973 to 300 in 1983.

Hawaiian geese were nearly wiped ▶ out by hunting, loss of habitat and competition from introduced species. They have been bred in captivity since 1949 and there are now more than 2,000 in reserves around the world.

Chinese alligators may now be extinct in their ▶ native China, but after many years of study, scientists know how to help them breed in zoos.

The bald eagle is the national bird of the USA.

Baby Chinese alligator

◀ Bald eagles nearly died out from loss of habitat, hunting and poisoning. Captive breeding has helped their numbers to increase.

Captive plants

Rare plants can be grown from seeds in special gardens. They can then be put back into the wild.

In Wales, 50 tufted saxifrage plants have been put back into the wild. They were grown from the seeds of the only two plants left in the area.

Safety in numbers

It is very difficult to build up numbers when there are very few members of a species left. Zoos around the world keep details of all their animals on computer and work together to match animals and help them breed.

Embryo transfer

To help species increase in number faster than they could naturally, a method called embryo transfer can be used. Scientists take an embryo (a tiny unborn animal) from a rare species and put it into the body of a similar common species. When the embryo is fully grown, the new mother gives birth to the rare species.

Przewalski's horses are extinct in the wild. This baby one was the result of embryo transfer. His mother is a New Forest pony.

Success stories

It usually takes more than one type of action to protect an endangered species, as you can find out below. All these species have faced extinction, but are now being helped to build up their numbers again.

Peace for polar bears

In the 1960s, polar bears were in danger of dying out. 1000 a year were being killed for skins and for sport. Scientists from Canada, the USA, Norway, Denmark and the USSR worked together to find the best way of saving them. In 1975, the five countries agreed to control hunting and protect the bears' habitats.

Polar bears are the largest bears in the world. There are now about 40,000 of them in the wild.

Victory for vicuñas

In South America, vicuñas were killed for their fine wool which is very valuable. By 1965, only 6,000 were left. In 1967, Peru set aside a reserve for the vicuñas. Two years later, four countries agreed to ban hunting and stop selling the wool. Now there are over 100,000 vicuñas in the wild.

Vicuñas are related to camels.

Welcome for whales

So many grey whales were killed, that they were nearly extinct by 1920. Since the 1940s they have been protected and their numbers have slowly built up. Today, over 8,000 visit the Pacific coast every winter to breed.

Grey whales breed near the Pacific coast of Mexico.

Action for alligators

American alligators were endangered by the draining of their marsh habitat and hunting for skins. By 1969, a population of over 10 million had been reduced to 600,000.

American alligator

In 1969, it became illegal to sell the skins. Now the number of alligators has increased to several million.

Koalas come back

There were once millions of koalas in Australia. Hunting and loss of habitat nearly made them extinct. Two million were killed for their skins in 1924.

Since the 1950s, koalas have been protected. Safe homes in wildlife parks have also helped them to make a comeback.

Overhunted otters

Southern sea otters were hunted for their very valuable fur. By 1914 just 14 were left. These were carefully protected. A ban on hunting and a safe place to live have now helped them build up numbers to about 1000.

Southern sea otters live off the coast of California.

Sea otters break open shellfish by smashing them on stones balanced on their chests.

In the 1950s, huge numbers of European river otters were killed by hunters and pesticides. Now hunting is banned and safer pesticides are used. The otters are just beginning to increase in numbers again.

River otter

Successful swans

Trumpeter swans

Millions of trumpeter swans were shot for their feathers. By the 1930s only 100 were left, even though hunting was banned in 1918.

In 1935, a reserve in the USA was set aside for the swans to breed. They have bred fast and there are now more than 10,000 in the wild.

Tortoise triumphs

People have been working hard to help the Galapagos giant tortoises. They have removed many of the goats, pigs and other animals which threaten the tortoises (see page 12). They also collect tortoise eggs, hatch babies in captivity and then release them into the wild.

Whoopers are winning

Whooping cranes nearly became extinct because of hunting and the draining of their marsh homes. By 1944, only 21 were left.

Whoopers usually lay two eggs, but only bring up one chick. Scientists help them breed by using sandhill cranes as foster parents. They put the extra egg into a sandhill crane's nest. The new parents bring up the chick as their own.

There are now over 200 whooping cranes.

Laws and agreements

There are many laws and agreements between countries to protect endangered species.

The most important is called the Convention on International Trade in Endangered Species (CITES). This is an agreement between over 100 countries to control the buying and selling of endangered species and things made from them.

Many groups try to get governments to pass more laws to protect species. You can find out more about this on page 22.

21

Getting involved

These are some ideas for more things you can do to help wildlife, in your area and around the world. Thousands of species of plants and animals are in danger of extinction and need our help now. Everybody can get involved in working to protect them.

Conservation groups

There are many groups which work to protect species. They spread information and raise money for projects. Some try to get new laws passed to ban hunting, trading and so on.

WWF – World Wide Fund for Nature

The WWF was set up in 1961 to make people aware of conservation problems and raise money to protect threatened species and habitats around the world. They run educational projects all over the world and have members in many countries.

The giant panda is the symbol of the WWF.

Operation Tiger (see page 14) was one of the WWF's most successful projects.

For more information write to:
Information Division, WWF International, Avenue du Mont-Blanc, CH-1196 Gland, Switzerland.

IUCN – International Union for Conservation of Nature

The IUCN has members in 120 countries. Its teams of experts gather information and work out the best way to protect species.

The IUCN Red List of Threatened Animals lists all known endangered species.

Greenpeace

Greenpeace often carry out brave acts to help save wildlife. One of their most famous campaigns is to save whales. It has helped get many people interested in trying to stop whales being killed.

ICBP – International Council for Bird Preservation

The ICBP works to save birds from extinction. You can join their World Bird Club and raise money for their Parrot Fund.

ICBP
32 Cambridge Rd.
Girton
Cambridge,
CB3 0PJ UK

Helping bats

Bats all over the world are endangered. To find out how you can help to protect them, write to:

Bat Conservation International,
P.O Box 162603,
Austin,
Texas 78716,
USA.

Zoos

Zoos help endangered species by research and captive breeding (see page 18). Many have activities and clubs for children. At some you can 'adopt' an animal. Get in contact with your nearest zoo and find out how you can get involved.

Zoos are good places to watch and learn about animals.

Buying souvenirs and presents

If you buy things made from many kinds of animals or plants, you add to the danger of them becoming extinct. These are some of the things you should avoid buying and tell other people not to buy.

Bags, wallets, belts, shoes and purses made from the skins of lizards, snakes, alligators and crocodiles

Stuffed turtles and tortoises, turtle soup, whole shells and turtle wax or oil

Ivory carvings, jewellery and other things made from tusks or horns

Endangered cacti and orchid plants

Feathers, wild birds' eggs, stuffed birds

Key fobs, toys, and other things made from real fur or skin

Hats, rugs, coats and other things made from the skins of big cats such as leopards and ocelots.

Other ideas

★Visit reserves, bird sanctuaries and botanical gardens to see rare species.

★Put up bat boxes and bird boxes. Bats and birds all over the world have suffered from loss of places to breed.

Thousands of people in the USA have helped bluebirds by putting up nesting boxes for them.

★Put out food and water for birds, especially in winter. If you start to do this, you should carry on all winter.

Good food for birds

Baked potatoes

Unsalted nuts in plastic net bags will attract small birds.

Bones

Cheese

Seeds

Fat

Apples

Remember

Our survival depends on the world around us. Every species is part of that world. We cannot continue to destroy our own living space and the animals and plants that share it with us. You can help make a difference.

Facts and records

Species knowledge

★Scientists believe there are between 5 and 30 million species on Earth, but they have only discovered and named 1.6 million.

★Between 5,000 and 10,000 new species are discovered every year.

★The disappearance of one plant species can cause the extinction of up to 30 species of animals.

Wonderful whales

★Blue whales (see page 11) are the largest animals in the world and also the largest that have ever lived. They weigh more than 20 male African elephants and can grow to 30m(33yds) long. Their eyes are the size of footballs and their tongues weigh the same as an elephant.

★Sperm whales come to the surface of the sea to breathe, but can stay underwater for almost two hours. They are the deepest diving animals, going as deep as 3,000m(3,280yds) down to look for food.

Incredible journeys

★Every autumn, grey whales (see page 20) travel nearly 10,000km(6,214 miles) from the Arctic to the coast of Mexico. The journey takes about 90 days. They return in the spring.

★Arabian oryx (see page 18) do not need to drink at all except when pregnant. One pregnant female walked 45km(28 miles) in a night, just for a drink of water.

Fussy eaters

★Koalas (see page 20) will only eat the leaves of five out of 350 kinds of eucalyptus trees.

The largest

★African elephants (see page 10) are the largest land animals and the largest plant-eating animals. The biggest ever recorded was about 4m(4.4yds) tall and weighed about the same as 16 cars.

★Polar bears (see page 20) are the largest meat-eating animals. Some are over 3m(3.3yds) tall when standing up on two legs.

★Cane toads (see page 13) are the world's largest toads. One female weighed over 2.3kg(5lb).

The smallest

★Bumblebee bats in Thailand are the smallest mammals. They weigh about 2g(0.07oz) and are the size of big butterflies.

★The tiny bee hummingbird of Cuba is the world's smallest bird. Adult males are only 57mm (2.2in) long, including their beaks and tails.

The fastest

★Peregrine falcons (see page 9) are the fastest animals. They can reach 350km(218 miles) per hour when swooping from a great height.

★Cheetahs (see page 10) are the fastest mammals. They can run at over 100km(62 miles) per hour for short distances.

The slowest

★Three-toed sloths (see page 8) are the slowest land mammals. On the ground they take a minute to travel 2m(2.2yds). In the trees they can speed up to 4.5m(5yds) a minute. They spend over three-quarters of their lives asleep.

Smelly flowers

★Rafflesia, the world's largest flower (see page 9) stinks of rotten meat.

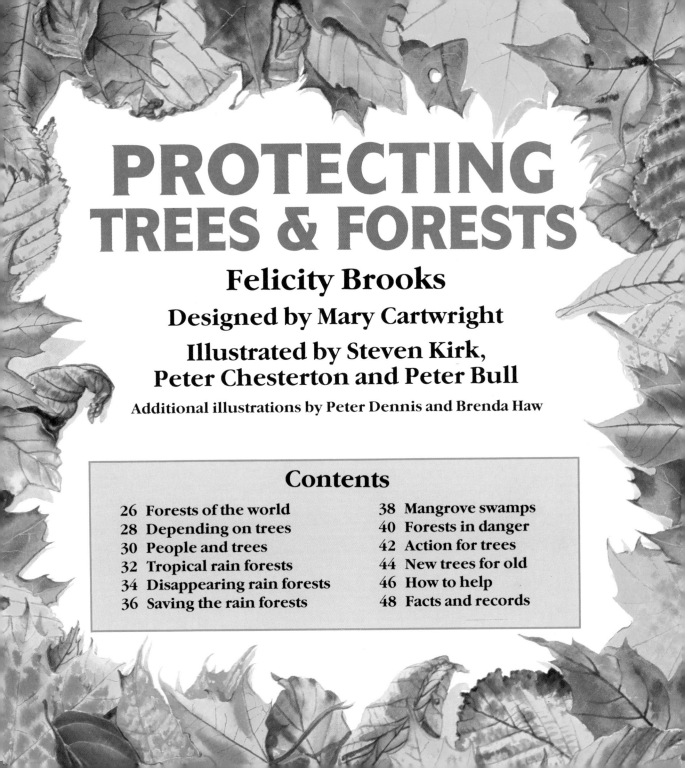

PROTECTING TREES & FORESTS

Felicity Brooks

Designed by Mary Cartwright

**Illustrated by Steven Kirk,
Peter Chesterton and Peter Bull**

Additional illustrations by Peter Dennis and Brenda Haw

Contents

Forests of the world

10,000 years ago, when people first started farming, huge forests covered about half of the Earth's land. Now less than a third of the land is covered in forests. Different types of forests grow in different parts of the world.

Types of forest

The type of forest which grows naturally in an area depends on the climate. Some trees grow best in cool parts of the world. Others can only grow in hot, rainy areas. This map shows the different climate areas and the kinds of trees which grow there.

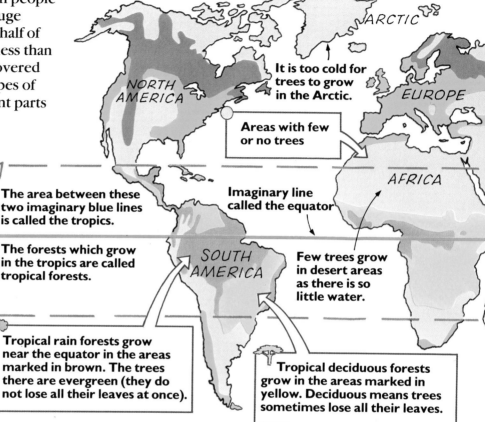

ARCTIC

NORTH AMERICA

EUROPE

AFRICA

SOUTH AMERICA

It is too cold for trees to grow in the Arctic.

Areas with few or no trees

The area between these two imaginary blue lines is called the tropics.

Imaginary line called the equator

The forests which grow in the tropics are called tropical forests.

Few trees grow in desert areas as there is so little water.

Tropical rain forests grow near the equator in the areas marked in brown. The trees there are evergreen (they do not lose all their leaves at once).

Tropical deciduous forests grow in the areas marked in yellow. Deciduous means trees sometimes lose all their leaves.

Tree groups

The world's trees can be divided into three main groups.

Broadleaved trees, such as sweet chestnuts, have wide flat leaves. Most are deciduous. Their wood is called hardwood.

A broadleaved tree's seeds are covered in a case of some type. It may be soft, hard or even prickly.

Conifers, such as firs, have needle or scale-shaped leaves. Most conifers are evergreen. Their wood is called softwood.

Needle-shaped leaves

Conifer seeds are found between the scales of cones.

Palm trees, such as date palms, grow in warm climates. Some even grow in the desert.

Palms do not have branches. Their huge leaves grow straight out of their trunks.

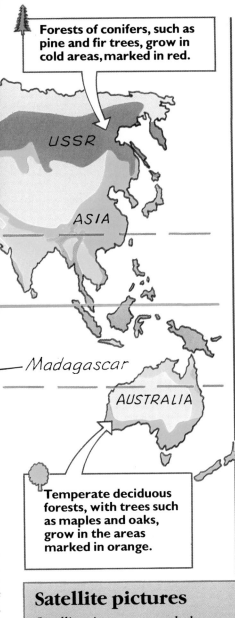

Forests of conifers, such as pine and fir trees, grow in cold areas, marked in red.

USSR

ASIA

Madagascar

AUSTRALIA

Temperate deciduous forests, with trees such as maples and oaks, grow in the areas marked in orange.

Disappearing forests

Many forests have already disappeared. As the number of humans has grown, billions of trees have been cut down to provide wood and land for farms and buildings.

In the richer areas of the world, many forests have been cut down in the past 500 years. In some areas (such as Europe and the USA) forests are now getting bigger, as more trees are planted.

Tropical forests

Most tropical forests are now disappearing fast. Half of the rain forests have already been cut down, mostly very recently. This is what has happened on the island of Madagascar.

Half of the USA was covered in forests when the first white settlers arrived in 1620.

USA

Areas of forest left by 1942

Now between a quarter and a third of the land is covered in forests.

Some farmland has been replanted with trees.

Original size of rain forest

Half of the rain forest had been cut down by 1950.

Today less than a third of the rain forest still exists.

MADAGASCAR

Satellite pictures

Satellites in space now help scientists to find out how much forest has disappeared. The information they send back is used to build up pictures of the Earth's surface.

Forests show up as red areas on satellite pictures.

Landsat Earth resources satellite

27

Depending on trees

Trees provide food and shelter for an enormous number of animals and plants. Different kinds of wildlife live in different types of forests. Few species survive when forests are destroyed.

Deciduous forests

These are some of the animals and plants that live in deciduous forests in Europe. Each species has its own living area and way of finding food.

Wildlife facts

★A small oak forest can provide homes for over 4,000 species of insects, birds and plants.

★Tropical forests contain by far the most species. 41,000 species of insects were found in a small patch of forest in Peru.

★A conifer forest supports six to ten species of birds. A mixed deciduous forest of the same size can support three times more.

Night Life

Some animals only come out at night. These are some of them.

Eagle owls are the largest, most powerful European owls. They can even kill roe deer.

Pipistrelle bat

Badger

Dormouse

Lobster moth

Beech trees are common in European forests.

Jay

Sparrowhawk

Bluebells

Roe deer live in family groups.

Oak

Brown bears are now rare. Some are still found in parts of France, Spain, Poland, Italy and Greece. They eat mainly fruit, leaves and insects.

Wild boars sniff out roots, bulbs, fungi and small animals to eat.

Woodpeckers find insects to eat by pecking holes in trees.

Nuthatches can run up and down tree trunks. They nest in holes in trees.

Woodsorrel

Common shrew

Red squirrel

Ivy

Dog's mercury

Hedgehog

Woodmouse

Speckled wood butterfly

Fly orchid

Stag beetles

Longhorn beetle

Lichen

Insects and fungi live on rotting logs.

Homes for birds

Many birds depend on trees. Each species has its own way of finding food. A North American wood of aspen and willow can support 12 species of small birds. Here are some of them.

Hummingbirds fly from flower to flower, feeding on nectar.

Flycatchers catch butterflies and other flying insects.

Traill's flycatcher

Flickers search for insects under the bark of trees.

Common flicker

Bluebirds sit on branches and drop to the ground to catch large insects.

Wrens hide in the bushes searching for insects.

House wren

Sparrows eat small seeds.

Chipping sparrow

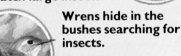

American robins look for worms and beetles on the ground.

Conifer forests

Conifer forests which have grown naturally contain more wildlife than those planted by humans (see below right). These are some of the species which live in a natural Scots pine wood.

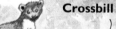

Long-eared owl

Crossbill

Pine marten

Goldcrest

Red deer

Capercaillies are shy forest birds. They fly up to branches to feed on leaves, buds, fruit, berries and insects.

Bilberry

Tree creeper

Fly agaric toadstool

Heather

Insects and trees

Many species of insects depend on trees. Native trees (ones that grow naturally in an area) support more species than trees brought from other countries.

A larch in its native Russia is home to 44 species of insects. In Britain, it only supports 17.

A willow in its native Britain shelters 266 insect species. In Russia, only 147 are found.

Unwelcoming trees

Many conifer forests have been specially planted by humans to provide wood. The trees are planted close together and are all the same age. This type of forest (called a plantation) does not support much wildlife.

Tall trees, all the same height, block out light so few plants can grow on the ground.

A thick layer of needles on the ground also stops plants growing.

There are no bushes to shelter insects so there is little food for birds.

Fallen trees are cleared away so there are no rotten logs for insects and fungi.

People and trees

Early people depended on trees for shelter, fuel, food and tools. Today, thousands of years later, we still cannot survive without them. They provide us with wood, food, paper and many other things. They keep soil in place and even help to keep the air clean.

Wonderful wood

Wood has a huge number of different uses. It can be cut and shaped to make all sorts of things. These are just a few of them.

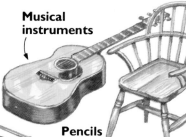

Musical instruments

Pencils

Boats

Furniture

Buildings

Look around you. What other things are made from wood?

Paper

Most paper is made in large factories from tiny fibres of wood. The wood comes from fast-growing trees such as conifers and eucalyptus.

Forests of eucalyptus are specially planted to grow wood for paper.

Recycling paper

Papermaking uses a lot of power as well as chemicals which pollute our world. Recycling paper (turning waste paper back into new paper) saves power, chemicals and wood so it helps protect the world.

Paper facts

★People in Europe use over 50 million tonnes (55 million tons) of paper every year.

★One edition of a daily newspaper uses wood from 5,000 trees.

★In richer countries, each person uses about two trees' worth of paper every year.

Useful trees

Many foods come from trees.

Mangoes, oranges, pears, apples, figs and cherries grow on trees.

Bananas grow in large bunches on banana trees.

Coconuts and dates grow on palm trees.

Chocolate is made from the seeds of cocoa trees.

Many types of nuts come from trees.

Cinnamon is the bark of cinnamon trees.

Walnuts

Hazel-nuts

These spices come from the seeds of trees.

Pepper

Nutmeg

Mace

Brazil nuts

Cloves are the dried buds of a tree.

These are some other things that come from trees.

Maple syrup from maple trees

Cork from the bark of cork oaks

Rubber from rubber trees

Chewing gum from chicle trees.

Fuel

Over half of all the wood used each year is burnt as fuel for cooking and heating. Half the people in the world use wood as their only fuel.

Nine out of ten meals in India are cooked on wood fires.

In many areas, too many trees have been cut down for firewood and no new trees have been planted. This causes problems for people who rely on firewood and also harms the environment (see right).

Trees and air

Trees help provide fresh air. They take in a gas called carbon dioxide and give off oxygen (which we need to breathe). Trees also help clean air by trapping dust in their leaves, so they are very useful in cities.

A small beech forest can trap 5 tonnes (5.5 tons) of dust a year.

Trees and the environment

This is what can happen when too many trees are cut down.

Soil loss

Tree roots bind soil together and help hold it in place. When forests are cleared, especially on hills, the top layer of soil is easily washed off the land by wind and rain.

The land soon becomes useless for farming. Deep cracks appear in the ground. Landslides and mudslides happen more often.

Land in Ethiopia after trees were cut down for firewood.

Floods

After trees have been cut down, a lot of soil is washed into rivers. It starts to block them up. This means that when there is heavy rain, the rivers overflow and flood.

This is what is happening in India, Nepal and Bangladesh.

Half of Nepal's forest has been cut down since 1956.

Area where trees have been cut down

Soil washed off land blocking up the river

Flooding

Nepal

Himalayas

Bangla-desh

River Ganges

250,000 tonnes (275,000 tons) of soil are washed into the Ganges from Nepal every year.

India

The Bay of Bengal is filling up with soil.

Bay of Bengal

The Ganges overflows often, causing terrible floods in Bangladesh.

Tropical rain forests

Over half of all the different kinds of animals and plants in the world live in tropical rain forests. The forests are also home to millions of people. They provide wood, food and many other things. They even help to make it rain.

Tropical rain forests grow in warm, rainy areas near the equator. The biggest is the Amazon rain forest in South America.

North America

Central America

Equator

Amazon

South America

Africa

Europe

Asia

India

South-east Asia

Australia

• Areas of rain forest

Rain forests of South-east Asia

The rain forests of South-east Asia are about 70 million years old. They are home to a great variety of animals and plants. Here are a few of them.

Wild Asian elephants live in the forests. They are smaller than African elephants.

Pitcher plants trap insects inside containers which grow on the ends of their leaves. They use the insects as food.

Orang-utans move slowly through the lower branches of the forests eating leaves, bark, nuts and fruit. Orang-utan means 'man of the woods'.

Tarsiers only come out at night. They have very large eyes and can move their heads right around to look behind them.

This colourful weevil lives in rain forests in New Guinea.

Flying lizards have flaps of skin on each side of their bodies. These can open up so the lizards can glide from tree to tree.

The tallest trees have wide roots called buttress roots. These help to keep them upright.

None of these species can survive when their rain forests are destroyed.

Living in the forest

Tribes of people have been living in rain forests for about 40,000 years. They fish, hunt animals, gather food and grow vegetables. They use thousands of different plants as medicines and get everything else they need from the forest. They know how to use the forest without harming it.

Mbuti pygmies

The Mbuti pygmies in West Africa live in groups of between 20 to 100 people. Each group agrees to hunt only in a certain area.

The Mbuti use bows and arrows or nets and spears to hunt. They also collect fruit and honey from the forest.

The Yanomami

The Yanomami are the largest tribe left in the Amazon. They hunt, fish and gather food. They also grow food in small gardens.

About 20 Yanomami families live in a building called a Yano. The Yanos are spaced far apart in the forest.

Rain forest facts

★There are about 400 types of trees in the forests of North America. There are over 2,000 in the tropical rain forest on the island of Madagascar.

★A quarter of all medicines are made from substances found in rain forest plants.

★The tiny tropical country of Panama in Central America has as many species of plants as the whole of Europe.

★Tribes in the Amazon rain forest know how to use more than 1,300 different types of plants as medicines.

Trees and water

A lot of the world's water comes from rain forests. Trees soak up rainwater from the soil. They release most of it back into the air from their leaves. This water goes to make more rain.

Clouds form from tiny drops of water joined together.

Water falls as rain from the clouds.

Roots take up water from the ground.

A lot of water is released back into the air from leaves.

Water shortage

When trees are cut down, rainwater runs away instead of going back into the air. In places where the rain forests have gone, it now rains less.

If all the forests disappear, a fifth of the world's people will not get as much water as they need to grow crops.

Disappearing rain forests

The world's tropical rain forests are disappearing fast. Half have already gone. Every minute, an area of rain forest about the size of fifteen football fields is destroyed or badly damaged. These are some of the different ways this happens.

Farming

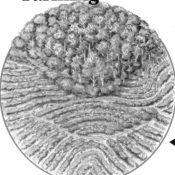

Large areas of forest are cut down and cleared to provide land for farming.

Some land is used to grow crops such as tea and coffee to sell to ◀ rich countries.

In Central and South America, a lot of land is used to graze cattle. This provides cheap meat for rich ▶ countries.

Cattle on rain forest land ⤹

Most rain forests are in poor countries. Many people there have no jobs or land. They move into a piece of forest, cut down trees, burn the plants and use the land to grow crops to eat.

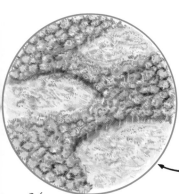

When the trees have gone, the soil soon becomes too poor to farm, so the farmers move on to destroy another piece of rain forest.

This 'slash and burn' farming is the main cause of rain forest destruction.

Mining

The search for oil and metals, such as iron and gold, also damages forests and makes people and animals homeless.

In Brazil, thousands of gold-miners have been digging in the Amazon rain forest. They cut down trees and make big holes in the ground. The waste from the mines pollutes rivers.

Gold-mine in the Amazon ⟶

Logging

People cut down big tropical trees, such as teak trees and sell the wood to rich countries. This damages the forest and scares away animals.

Most logging takes place in South-east Asia. ⟶

◀ Loggers make roads to get to the big trees. This lets farmers enter the forest. They start to destroy areas of forest, moving further and further away from the road.

Tribes in danger

Tribes who have been living in the forest for thousands of years are now in danger of being wiped out. They cannot survive when the forest is destroyed.

In Brazil, 1,500 Yanomami Indians have died since 1988. They have been poisoned and shot by gold-miners. They have also died from diseases, such as malaria, which the miners have brought in.

The damage to the forest and the pollution of the rivers have ruined the Yanomami's hunting and fishing, so many are starving. If the Yanomami are to survive, their land must be protected.

Tribe facts

★ About 1,000 tribes live in the rain forests around the world. Most are in danger of being wiped out.

★ 100 years ago, there were six million Indians in the Amazon rain forest. Now less than 100,000 survive.

★ 120 tribes in the Amazon rain forest have been wiped out since 1900.

★ Less than 9,000 Yanomami Indians are left in the Amazon rain forest.

★ Less than 200,000 pygmies remain in the African rain forests.

Trees and the weather

Burning forests causes unwelcome changes in the Earth's weather. Here you can find out how.

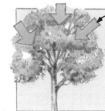

Growing trees soak up carbon dioxide (CO_2) from the air and use it to form wood.

When trees are burned, this CO_2 goes back into the air.

CO_2 and other gases build up above the Earth. They trap heat on the surface, acting like the glass in a greenhouse.

Most of the gases come from burning fuels such as coal and oil. Burning rain forests also releases two billion tonnes (over two billion tons) of CO_2 into the air each year.

Global warming

We now burn so much fuel and release so much CO_2 that too much heat is being trapped, making the Earth warm up.

This is called global warming. It upsets the world's weather. It will cause more floods, water shortages and storms.

Gases

Heat from the sun

Some heat still escapes through the gases.

More and more heat is being trapped by CO_2 and other 'greenhouse' gases.

35

Saving the rain forests

We must act now to save the rain forests. The survival of millions of plants, animals and people depends on it. These are some of the different ways the rain forests can be saved.

Forest reserves

A good way to save forests is to set aside areas such as national parks and reserves where plants and animals can live safely. There are now over 600 rain forest reserves, but many more are needed.

Cross River National Park in Nigeria covers 3,000km² (1,200 sq miles) of forest. The forest is about 60 million years old.

400 species of trees grow in the park. They protect the land from flooding and soil loss.

Three-quarters of Belize in Central America is still covered in forest. A third of the forest is protected.

Jaguars are one of the species that live in Cockscomb Basin Wildlife Sanctuary in Belize.

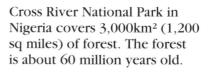

Buffer zones

For reserves to work well, they must not upset the lives of local people. People must be able to earn a living from the forest. An area called a 'buffer zone' around a safe area allows them to do this.

Some farming, fishing, hunting and logging is allowed in the buffer zone.

Farming, fishing and so on are not allowed in this area. It protects a lot of wildlife.

BUFFER ZONE

Using the forest

Rain forest land is worth more if the trees are left standing than if they are cut down and the land is used for farming. Here are some ways of using forests without harming them.

Selective logging

◄ Selective logging means that people only remove certain trees to sell, rather than all the trees. This allows the forest to repair itself as it does when trees fall down naturally.

Forests for tourists

Visitors bring money to an area when they come to visit forest reserves.

100,000 people visit Kinabalu Park in Malaysia each year. They can watch animals from walkways built in the trees.

In safe hands

In Colombia, 18 million hectares (44 million acres) of forest has been given to 70,000 Indians. This area will be safe, as the Indians know how to look after it.

An area of forest almost as big as New Zealand is now protected.

Colombia is in South America

Yellow areas show national parks.

Forest belonging to Indians

SOUTH AMERICA

COLOMBIA

Amazon rain forest

Debt for nature

Many tropical countries have borrowed money from rich countries. Now they are cutting down their forests to make money to repay these debts.

A way of stopping this happening is for the rich countries to agree to wipe out some of the debts. In return, the tropical countries must set aside areas of forest as reserves. These are called debt-for-nature swaps.

Sharing land

Many poor farmers destroy forests because they have no other land. In Brazil, for example, a few rich people own half the land but 12 million people own no land at all.

Land needs to be shared more fairly, so that poor people will not need to destroy the forests.

Brazil

Farms in the forest

The Chagga people have been farming in the rain forest in Africa for hundreds of years. Their methods, which do not harm the forest, are now being studied by experts.

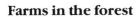

The Chagga cut down a few trees, but leave most standing. They then grow bananas and other foods.

Extractive reserves

In extractive reserves, people can take out nuts, plants, fruit, rubber and so on. The amount they take is controlled so the forest is not damaged.

Collecting rubber in Acre Province in Brazil

Medicines

Scientists are now learning from forest people which plants can be used in medicines. These will add to the medicines we already use that are made from rain forest plants.

In the future, people with AIDS may be helped by a drug made from the seeds of Moreton Bay chestnuts. The chestnuts grow in Australian rain forests.

37

Mangrove swamps

Mangrove trees grow in and near the tropics. There are about 70 different kinds. They are found in muddy swamps along coasts and near where rivers come out into the sea.

Other trees cannot survive in these wet, salty places but mangroves are well suited to them. They can also survive the changes in the water level as the tide goes in and out.

Map showing areas where mangroves grow: North America, South America, Africa, India, South-east Asia, Australia. Areas where mangroves grow.

Roots for breathing

Most trees can only grow in soil which has air spaces in it. Mangroves can grow in mud which has little air in it because of their special 'breathing' roots. These grow above the mud and take in oxygen from the air. The oxygen passes down to other roots buried in the mud.

Level of water at high tide

Black mangroves have 'tube roots' which stick out of the mud at low tide.

Level of water at low tide

Some types of mangroves have 'knee roots'. These loop out of the mud and back in again.

Red mangroves have 'prop roots'. These grow in an arch out from their trunks.

Prop roots help hold the trees in place as water flows in and out. They also trap mud and sand.

Animals of the mangroves

These are some of the unusual animals which live in the mangrove swamps.

Crab-eating macaques spend most of their time in the trees. At low tide, they search the mud for crabs and other small animals to eat.

Archer fish shoot down insects by squirting jets of water out of their mouths.

A lot of crabs live in the swamps. Male fiddler crabs have one huge orange claw.

Mudskippers are fish that can live on land and in water. They move around on the mud at low tide and can even climb tree trunks.

The mangroves provide homes for many birds. Scarlet ibis live in the swamps in Central and South America.

Mangroves in danger

In many countries, large areas of mangroves are being destroyed. Many animals are losing their homes. These are some of the ways this happens.

The trees are cut down ▶ and the land is used to grow crops such as rice.

◀ Whole areas are cleared, so the wood can be used for fuel and building.

The trees are cut down ▶ and the swamps are drained and filled in. Then houses, factories and roads are built.

Houses in Florida, USA, built on land that was once a mangrove swamp

◀ The trees are killed by pollution when oil from ships at sea is washed on to the shore.

These mangroves in Indonesia died when the mud was polluted with oil.

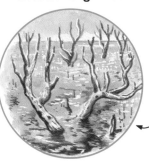

Oil wells are built in ▶ the swamps, killing many trees and polluting the mud.

Oil well in a mangrove swamp in Nigeria

Protecting the mangroves

If people look after the trees and do not cut down too many at the same time, forests of mangroves can be useful and valuable. This is how people in the Matang Mangrove Forest Reserve in Malaysia look after the mangroves.

The forest is divided up ▶ into small areas. Only a few areas at a time are cleared. The wood is used for fuel.

The areas will not be ▶ cleared again for 40 years. New trees have time to grow. Trees are planted if they do not grow naturally.

Every few years, the ▶ trees are thinned out. The extra wood is used by local builders.

2,000 people work in ▶ the forest. 10,000 others live by selling fish, shellfish and prawns from the swamp.

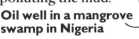

Forests in danger

It is not only tropical forests which need to be saved. There are dangers to trees in other parts of the world. These are some of them.

Pollution

Pollution kills animals and plants, damages buildings and poisons water. It can also harm people's health. The worst type for trees is called acid rain. It destroys large areas of forest. This is how acid rain forms.

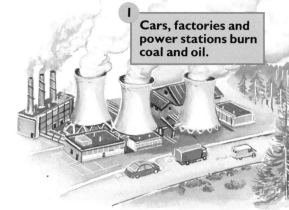

2 Waste gases are sent out into the air in smoke and fumes.

1 Cars, factories and power stations burn coal and oil.

3 Some of the gas damages nearby trees. It attacks the surface of their leaves.

More threats to trees

◀ Forest fires kill millions of trees every year. China has the worst forest fires. In 25 years it has lost an area of forest the size of Spain and Italy put together.

◀ Big storms can kill millions of trees. This is what Hurricane David did to forests on the island of Dominica.

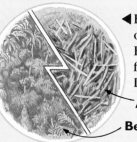

After hurricane

Before hurricane

Diseases wipe out many ▶ trees. Dutch elm disease killed 25 million elms in England and Wales.

Ancient woods have been ▶ replaced by plantations (see page 29). Woodland butterflies, such as purple emperors, are now rare because of this.

◀ Many trees are cut down to provide land for things such as roads and buildings.

Old forest being cut down to make way for a road.

◀ Some people damage trees on purpose. They break off the tops of young trees or carve into the bark of older trees. Carving the bark may kill a tree.

Travelling pollution

Pollution can travel a long way, so countries which make a lot of it may not be the ones which suffer the most damage.

Each year 3 million tonnes (3.3 million tons) of acid pollution are blown into Canada from the USA.

CANADA

Trees in Canada, such as maples, are damaged by acid rain from the USA.

USA

4 Some waste gas mixes with tiny drops of water in the air, forming harmful substances called acids.

5 Acid pollution may be carried a long way by the wind before falling as acid rain or snow.

6 Some acid rain falls on to trees.

7 Some acid rain falls on to rivers and lakes.

8 Some falls on to soil and is taken up by trees through their roots.

Acid rain damage

Acid rain makes trees weak so that they are easily attacked by insect pests or diseases. Conifers, silver birches and beeches suffer the most damage from acid rain.

Conifer damaged by acid rain

Yellow spots appear on the needles.

The tree loses many needles.

The tops and tips of branches start to die.

The roots become weak and cannot take up enough water from the soil.

Whole forests have died because of acid rain. Over half of Germany's forests are now damaged or dying.

An area of the Black Forest in 1970

The same area today

Acid rain facts

★ Europe and North America have the worst acid rain problem. It also falls in Mexico, Australia, China, Japan and many other places.

★ In Austria, if nothing is done, scientists believe there will be no trees left by 1997.

★ Rain in Europe now contains up to 80 times more acid than in 1950.

Farm alarm

Farmers cut down trees and hedges to make big fields which are easier to look after with modern machines.

Wandoo forests in Australia were cut down to make way for wheat fields. 15 kinds of animals were wiped out in the area because of this.

Over 6,000km (3,700 miles) of hedges are removed in England every year.

Action for trees

Trees take a long time to grow but can be cut down quickly. We must act now to protect as many trees as possible for the future and stop so many from being destroyed. These are some ways this can be done.

In parts of Africa, women have to walk 10km (6 miles) every day to find wood.

Safe areas

Places such as nature reserves and national parks provide safe homes for plants and animals. They are also interesting places to visit.

The last giant redwood trees are protected in the Redwood National Park in California, USA.

Hackfall Wood in England is over 350 years old. It contains oak, ash, beech, wild cherry and Scots pine. It has been protected since 1989.

Trees for fuel

In many countries firewood is scarce and expensive. Families may spend a quarter of their money on it. Planting groups of trees especially for firewood helps stop old forests being cut down.

Village woodlots

◀ Village woodlots are small groups of trees planted near villages. Villagers plant the trees, look after them and use the wood for fuel when the trees have grown.

Seedlings are grown in plastic tubes before being planted.

Fuelwood plantations

A fuelwood plantation is a large area of fast-growing trees. It is ▶ planted as a crop especially for firewood. Every time trees are cut down, more are planted.

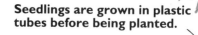

Plantation of eucalyptus trees in Lesotho, Africa

Using stoves

Open fires use a lot of wood and can be dangerous. A stove may use only a quarter of the wood needed for a fire, so using stoves helps to save trees.

Cooking pot

These stoves, called jikos, are now used in Kenya. They save thousands of trees a year.

Wood goes in here

Unusual action

These are some of the unusual ways people have found to stop trees being cut down.

Women and girls in a village in Northern India stopped a forest being cut down by hugging every tree the loggers wanted to fell. The women said the trees gave them 'soil, water and pure air'.

The idea of tree-hugging has spread and saved trees in other areas.

In Australia, people stopped an ancient forest from being cut down by burying themselves up to their necks in the road. This stopped the loggers' trucks reaching the forest.

Stopping acid rain

To protect trees from acid rain we need to cut down on the amount of pollution going into the air (see pages 40-41). These are some ways of doing this.

Power stations can clean ▶ smoke before it is released. This is expensive but it cuts pollution by nine tenths.

Exhaust fumes can be cleaned by fitting cars ◀ with a piece of equipment called a catalytic converter. Driving more slowly and less often also cuts down on pollution.

Cycling, walking and using buses and trains, instead of cars, helps to save energy and ▶ makes less pollution.

◀ Turning off heaters and lights and taking showers instead of baths saves fuel.

Cleaner fuel

There are ways of making energy without polluting the air. We need to switch to these methods to help stop acid rain.

Solar energy (energy from the sun) can be ▶ used to heat water and make electricity.

Solar energy station in France. —

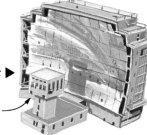

◀ Windmills use the power of the wind to make electricity.

Wind farm in the Netherlands

Dams on rivers are used to trap the energy of flowing water. Scientists are also ▶ trying to find ways of trapping the energy of waves.

Dam in the USA —

43

New trees for old

All around the world people are now planting more trees. Some plan to plant billions. These will form new forests or take the place of ones which have been destroyed. Planting a forest takes a lot of work, time and money. It is always better to save the ones we already have.

Canada's conifers

In Quebec in Canada, there are plans to plant 250 million trees a year to rebuild forests. Most will be conifers such as fir and pine trees.

Planting problems

Young trees must get plenty of water and be protected from strong winds and sun. Hungry animals must also be kept away. These are some of the different ways this can be done.

Shrubs with large thorns are planted to make a 'living fence' to keep out animals.

Ditches stop cattle and other large animals reaching trees.

Small stone walls are built around each tree.

'Growth tubes' protect trees and so help them to grow quickly.

Trees against pollution

The American Forestry Association plans to plant 100 million trees by 1993. These will soak up 18 million tonnes (20 million tons) of CO_2 from the air each year, helping to slow global warming.

Guanacaste Park

In Costa Rica, people are rebuilding a tropical forest in the Guanacaste National Park. They collect seeds, plant trees and put out fires. It may take 500 years before the forest is fully grown again.

Seeds from trees in the Guanacaste National Park

Forests for the future

Children around the world are helping to plant forests for the future. In Kenya in Africa and Gujarat in India, every school has a tree nursery where trees are grown from seeds. In Vietnam, children learn tree-planting in school.

Tree-planting in India

Forests for Brazil

A group of 12 people in Brazil have a plan to plant 10 billion trees in areas where forests have been destroyed. This is called the Floram Project. The new forests will provide wood and help stop global warming and soil loss.

Community forests

There are plans to plant 300 million deciduous trees in England and Wales. These will form 'community forests' near 20 towns. People from the towns will be able to go for walks in the forests.

Holding back the desert

More trees are planted each year in China than in any other country. There are plans to cover a fifth of the land with trees by the year 2000. At the moment a tenth is covered.

This 'Great Green Wall' of trees will help stop the Gobi Desert spreading further into China.

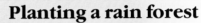

Gobi Desert

Planting a rain forest

Huge areas of Vietnam's rain forests and mangroves were destroyed in the Vietnam war. People there now plant 500 million trees a year to replace them. After 12 years' work, scientists have found ways of growing rain forest trees from seeds.

Young rain forest trees are sheltered from the fierce sun by large 'nurse trees'.

Green Belt Movement

Women in Kenya started the 'Green Belt Movement' to get people to plant trees. Over two million trees have now been planted. 15,000 farmers and half a million children are working on the project.

Tree nursery

Going for a billion

Australia has lost huge areas of forest since the first Europeans arrived 200 years ago. This includes three-quarters of its rain forests. There are now plans to plant one billion trees to help protect the soil.

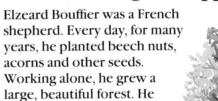

The man who grew happiness

Elzeard Bouffier was a French shepherd. Every day, for many years, he planted beech nuts, acorns and other seeds. Working alone, he grew a large, beautiful forest. He brought life back to an area where nothing grew and nobody lived.

Elzeard Bouffier is known as 'the man who planted trees and grew happiness'.

45

How to help

You can help plant trees for the future. You can also help to protect trees and forests in your area and around the world.

A great many trees are in danger and need our help now. These are some ideas for different things you can do to help.

Planting trees

Planting the right type of trees will help provide a habitat for wildlife and improve your local area. You can grow trees from seeds or buy saplings (young trees). Your trees will need a lot of time and care, so try to get a group of people to help.

Trees from seeds

Collect seeds from local trees in autumn and winter. The seeds should be firm and healthy. Damaged ones will not grow.

Healthy acorn from oak tree

Acorn damaged by insects

Beech nut

Maple seeds

Plant the seeds at a depth of 2-3cm (1 in) in damp compost. Protect the pots from strong heat and frost. Keep the compost damp.

Some seeds, such as acorns ▶ and beech nuts, may start growing in the spring. Other kinds may take longer, so be patient.

You can plant your seedlings outside when they are about 10cm (4 in) tall. They will need protection and plenty of water.

Plant your seedlings in a sheltered spot at least 15cm (6 in) apart.

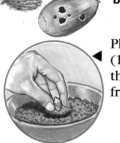

Remember to water your trees in dry weather.

When the trees are about 60cm (2 feet) tall, they can be planted out in their final position in early autumn (see right). ▶

Which trees to plant

Plant native trees (the kinds that grow naturally in your area). These will be best suited to the conditions and will shelter the most wildlife.

Where to plant

In gardens, school grounds or on local land. Get permission unless it is your land. Do not plant the trees too close to buildings as they will need room for their branches and roots to grow.

Small trees will grow well in tubs on balconies.

How long will it take?

The big trees in your area may be over 100 years old. It will be a long time before your trees are this big, but if you plant now, you can watch the trees grow as you grow up.

Planting a young tree

You will need:

Garden spade and fork

Young tree (grown from seed or bought)

Wooden stake

Adjustable rubber tie (available from a nursery or garden centre)

Mulch (wet straw, leaves, compost, manure)

Tree fact
★Each year, around the world, 11 million more hectares (27 million more acres) of trees are cut down than are planted.

Recycling paper

Recycling paper helps protect the environment (see page 30) and saves trees. Collect waste paper and cardboard at school and at home for recycling.

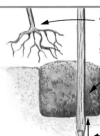

Paper and card with wax or plastic on it cannot be recycled.

Newspapers, magazines and envelopes can be recycled.

Find out who will take paper for recycling – try a paper merchant, or your local authority or conservation group.

Joining a group

Many conservation groups work to protect ancient forests and raise money to plant new trees. Try asking at your local library for information about groups you can join.

Organize a tree club

You could organize your own tree club with a group of friends. These are some ideas for things you could do.

Find out more ▶ about the trees that grow in your area.

Grow seeds and plant trees.

Raise money for groups which work to save tropical forests and other ancient forests.

Spread information about the importance of trees.

Other ideas

★Buy recycled paper and try to get your family to buy recycled kitchen towels, tissues and so on.

★Re-use old paper bags and envelopes.

★Don't buy things which come with a lot of packaging.

★Tell people not to buy furniture, souvenirs and other things made from tropical woods such as mahogany.

★Adopt a tree near your home. Watch it change through the seasons. Give it a bucket of water in dry weather. Let your local conservation group know if you think it is in danger.

The collar is where the roots meet the stem.

Push the stake into the soil at the bottom of the hole.

30cm (1 foot)

Dig a hole deep enough so that the tree can sit in it up to its collar and wide enough for all its roots. Break up the soil at the bottom of the hole.

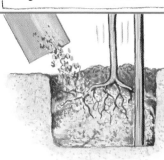

Soak the roots well and place the tree in the hole. Put some of the soil back in. Shake the tree gently as you add the soil, so it gets between the roots.

You can adjust the tie as the stem grows thicker.

A layer of mulch around the tree helps stop weeds growing. It also helps stop the soil drying out.

Tread the soil down and add some more. Keep doing this until the hole is full. Fix the tree to the stake with the tie. Water the tree well.

Facts and records

Record breakers

★African ironwood is the heaviest wood in the world. It sinks like stone in water.

★Maidenhair trees, or ginkgos, come from China and are now found in many parts of the world. Fossils show that these trees have been living on Earth for 250 million years.

★The tallest tree ever recorded was an Australian eucalyptus tree which measured over 132m (144yds) - about 75 times the height of an adult.

★A giant redwood tree called General Sherman in California, USA is the world's largest living thing. It is 84m(92yds) tall and 25m(27yds) round the trunk.

★A bristlecone pine in the White Mountains, USA is the oldest living tree. It is 4,700 years old.

Tree facts

★A large oak tree has about 250,000 leaves and can make 50,000 acorns a year.

★A fully - grown tree needs as much as 1,400 litres (365 gallons) of water on a hot summer's day.

★The fruit of billygoat plum trees in Australia contain more vitamin C than any other food.

Vanishing trees

★Half of the Netherlands' and a third of Switzerland's forests are dying because of acid rain.

★In India, 10 million trees are cut down every day. Most of the wood is burned as fuel.

★175,000km(107,000miles) of hedgerows across Britain have been removed in the past 40 years - enough to stretch almost 5 times around the world.

Tropical richness

★An area of tropical rain forest half the size of a football field contains up to 86 different types of trees. An area of European forest of the same size has about four.

★2,500 different species of birds live in tropical rain forests – almost a third of all known bird species.

Farmers for trees

★Between 1980 and 1985, over 22 million trees were planted on farms in England and Wales – an average of 240 trees per farm.

Using trees

★We now use enough wood every year to cover a city the size of Birmingham (the second largest city in England) to a depth of about 24m(26.5yds).

★1000 million trees are made into disposable nappies* each year.

★In Sweden, scientists have found a way of making 1000 nappies* from one tree. Before, less than half this number could be made.

★It takes 17 trees, 273,000 litres (71,000 gallons) of water and an enormous amount of electricity to produce one tonne (1.1 ton) of toilet paper.

★If we recycled half of the world's paper, it would save an area the size of Denmark from being used to grow trees just for paper.

★One tree can make a million matches. One match can destroy a million trees.

*diapers (US).

PROTECTING RIVERS & SEAS

Kamini Khanduri

Edited by Felicity Brooks

Designed by Mary Cartwright

Illustrated by Steven Kirk, Peter Chesterton and Peter Bull

Contents

Conservation consultant: Judy Oglethorpe

All about water

All living things need water to survive. On Earth, there is plenty. Water covers two-thirds of the planet's surface. The seas and oceans contain salt water. The rivers, lakes, streams and ponds contain fresh water. In this book, you can find out why the world's water is now in danger, and how we can protect it.

The planet Earth looks blue from space because there is so much water on it.

Pacific Ocean

The water cycle

There is no new water. The same water keeps moving between sea, air and land. This movement is called the water cycle. The picture below shows how it works.

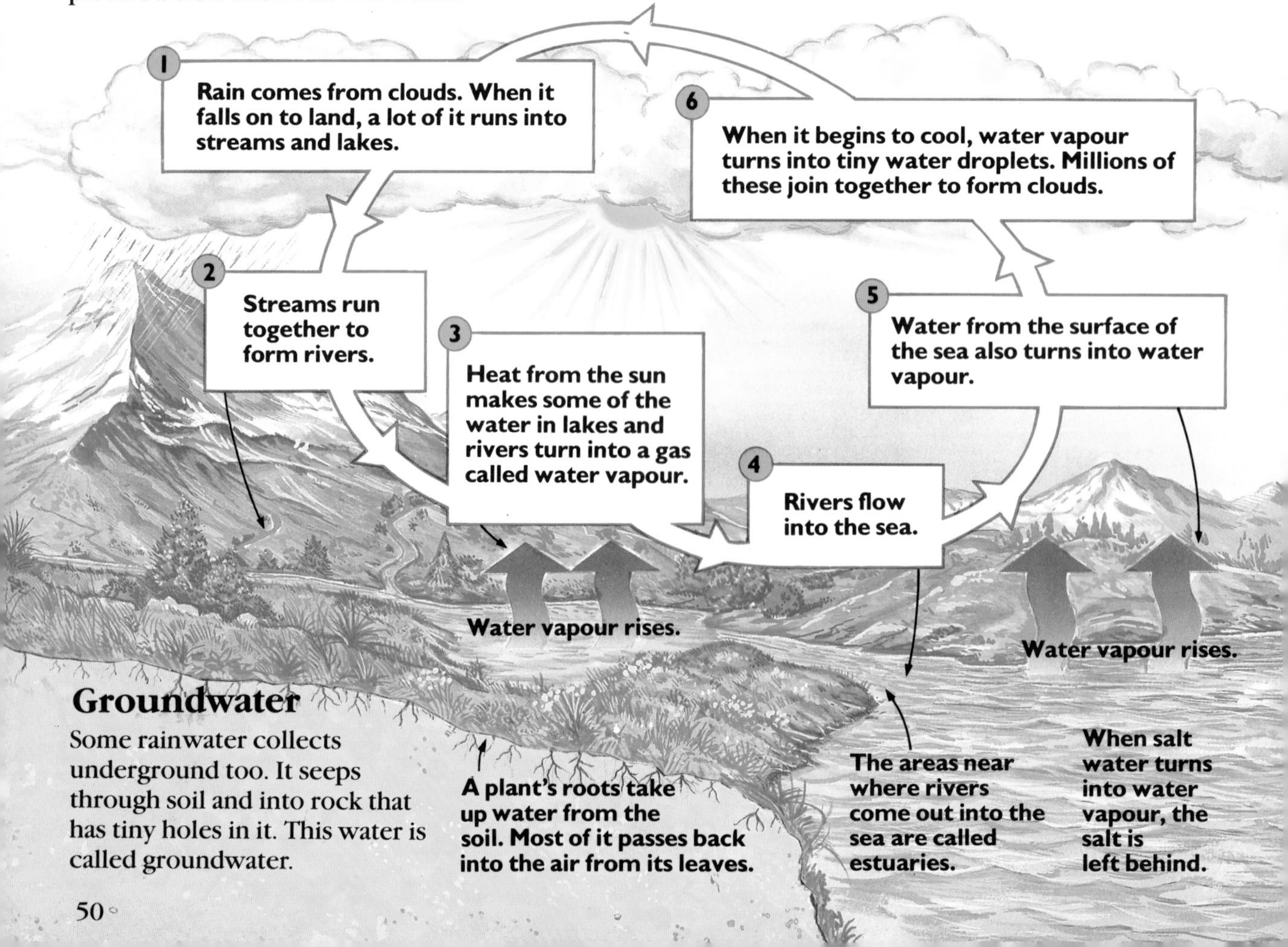

1 Rain comes from clouds. When it falls on to land, a lot of it runs into streams and lakes.

6 When it begins to cool, water vapour turns into tiny water droplets. Millions of these join together to form clouds.

2 Streams run together to form rivers.

3 Heat from the sun makes some of the water in lakes and rivers turn into a gas called water vapour.

5 Water from the surface of the sea also turns into water vapour.

4 Rivers flow into the sea.

Water vapour rises.

Water vapour rises.

Groundwater

Some rainwater collects underground too. It seeps through soil and into rock that has tiny holes in it. This water is called groundwater.

A plant's roots take up water from the soil. Most of it passes back into the air from its leaves.

The areas near where rivers come out into the sea are called estuaries.

When salt water turns into water vapour, the salt is left behind.

Living in water

Many plants and animals live in or near water. The place where a plant or animal lives is called its habitat. Below are some water habitats. You can find out about the wildlife living there on pages 52-57.

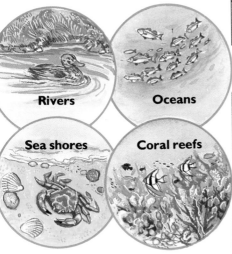

Rivers

Oceans

Sea shores

Coral reefs

Pollution

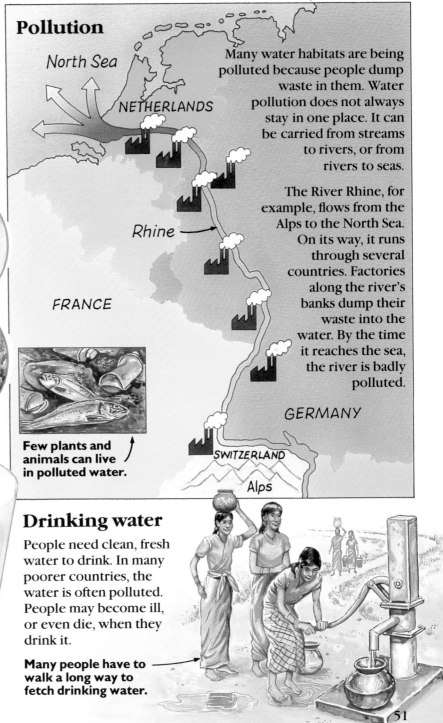

North Sea

NETHERLANDS

Rhine

FRANCE

GERMANY

SWITZERLAND

Alps

Few plants and animals can live in polluted water.

Many water habitats are being polluted because people dump waste in them. Water pollution does not always stay in one place. It can be carried from streams to rivers, or from rivers to seas.

The River Rhine, for example, flows from the Alps to the North Sea. On its way, it runs through several countries. Factories along the river's banks dump their waste into the water. By the time it reaches the sea, the river is badly polluted.

Water facts

★ Only a tiny amount of the Earth's water is fresh water. Most of this is under the ground, or frozen into ice.

★ Each person needs to drink about 1,000 litres (2,100 pints) of water a year.

★ Water makes up nearly three-quarters of a person's body weight.

Drinking water

People need clean, fresh water to drink. In many poorer countries, the water is often polluted. People may become ill, or even die, when they drink it.

Many people have to walk a long way to fetch drinking water.

51

Freshwater habitats

All kinds of wildlife live in or beside fresh water. Many are now in danger from pollution, and because their habitats are being destroyed by humans.

River homes

These are some of the animals and plants that live in or beside a European river. They are all suited, or adapted, to this habitat.

Wetlands

Wetlands are areas of land which are often covered by water. Swamps, marshes and estuaries are all wetlands. Wetlands are home to a great number of different kinds of plants and animals. Here are some of them.

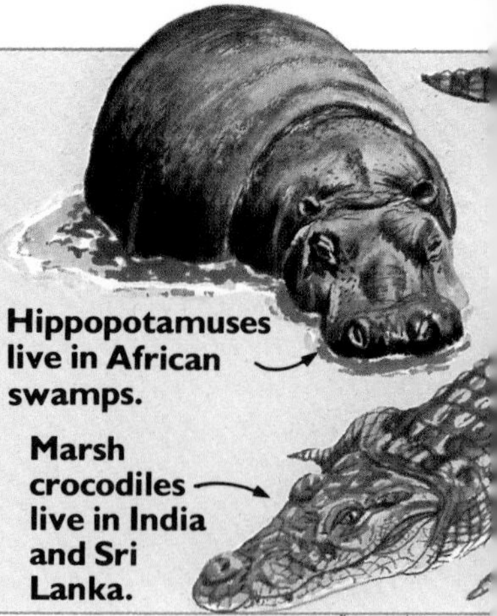

Hippopotamuses live in African swamps.

Marsh crocodiles live in India and Sri Lanka.

Dragonflies lay their eggs in water. After hatching, dragonfly nymphs stay in the water until they turn into adults.

Dragonfly nymph

Adult dragonfly

Reeds

Willow tree

Bulrushes

Kingfishers sit on branches above the water. They dive down to catch fish from the river below.

Otters live near water, in holes in the ground. They swim very well, and catch fish and other small animals, such as frogs.

Fish

Many kinds of fish live in fresh water. Different fish eat different things, so they are not all looking for the same food.

Carp eat insects.

Perch eat small fish.

Bitterling eat plants.

Salmon spend most of their lives in the sea but they swim up rivers to lay their eggs.

Wetland food chain

Stork

Many birds use wetlands as resting places on their long journeys.

In every habitat, animals and plants are linked by a food chain, with animals depending on plants, or on other animals, for food. Below you can see the way that some animals and plants are linked in a wetland food chain.

Cordgrass is eaten by freshwater shrimps.

Freshwater shrimps are eaten by eels.

Eels are eaten by storks.

Beavers

Beavers live in family groups, in Europe and North America. They build homes, called lodges, in streams and rivers. They also build dams, to widen the stream or river into a pond. This stops other animals from reaching the lodge, and harming the beavers.

Inside the lodge

Beavers' living area

Underwater food store

Lodge entrance

Lodge

Lodges and dams are made of sticks, stones and mud.

Dam

Beavers cut down trees with their sharp front teeth. They use the wood for building and the bark for food.

Frogs and toads

Frogs and toads live both in water and on land. Most lay their eggs in fresh water.

Golden toads are only found in Costa Rica, but none have been seen since 1989.

Pine Barrens tree frogs live in North American swamps. Their homes are now being destroyed.

Surinam toads carry their eggs on their backs, until they grow into tiny toads.

Eggs

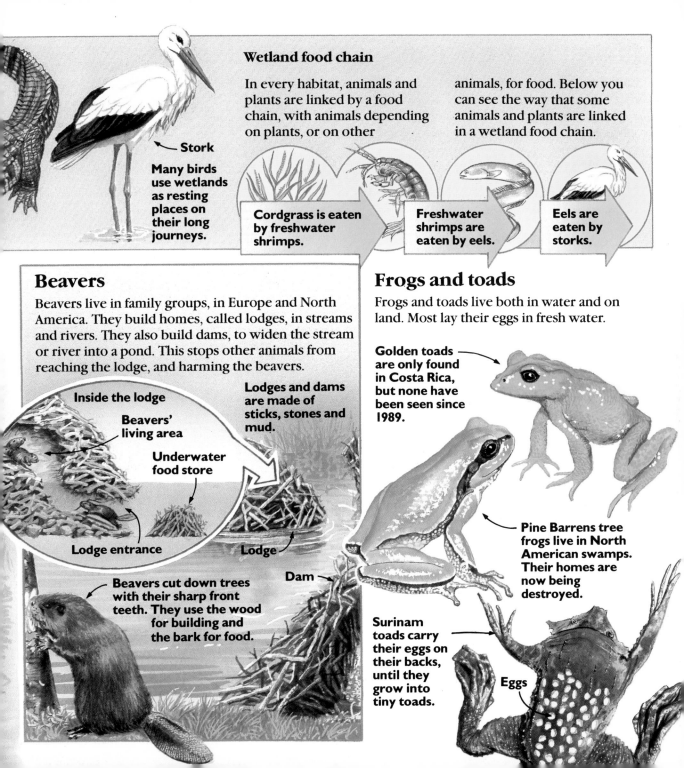

Living in the ocean

Seas and oceans are large areas of salt water. They make up nine-tenths of the water on Earth. Many animals living in seas and oceans are now in great danger from pollution of their habitats, and from hunting and fishing.

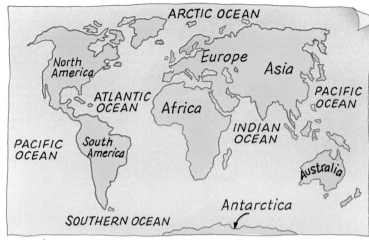

Cold-water animals

The Arctic and Southern Oceans contain very cold water. Here are some of the animals that are adapted to survive there.

Polar bears live in the Arctic Ocean, and on the ice there. They are very good swimmers. They feed on fish and seals.

White fur helps to keep polar bears hidden against the ice and snow.

Penguins cannot fly but they are excellent swimmers. This helps them to catch fish in the water.

Penguins use their narrow wings as flippers.

Seals cannot breathe underwater, but some can stay under for up to half an hour. Seals eat fish and shellfish.

A thick layer of fat under the skin keeps seals warm in icy water.

Living underwater

All kinds of creatures live underwater. Different animals live in different parts of the sea, from the surface down to the bottom.

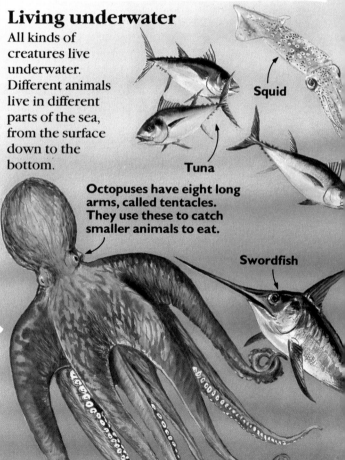

Squid

Tuna

Octopuses have eight long arms, called tentacles. They use these to catch smaller animals to eat.

Swordfish

54

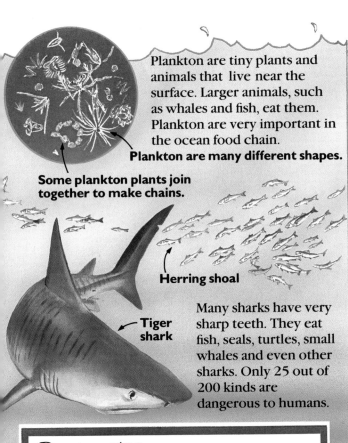

Plankton are tiny plants and animals that live near the surface. Larger animals, such as whales and fish, eat them. Plankton are very important in the ocean food chain.

Plankton are many different shapes.

Some plankton plants join together to make chains.

Herring shoal

Tiger shark

Many sharks have very sharp teeth. They eat fish, seals, turtles, small whales and even other sharks. Only 25 out of 200 kinds are dangerous to humans.

Whales

Whales live in the sea, but have to swim to the surface to breathe. There are more than 80 different kinds. Whales are very intelligent animals. Many of them are in danger from hunting and pollution.

Toothed whales, such as dolphins, eat squid and fish.

Baleen whales, such as humpback whales, have no teeth. They eat animal plankton.

They sieve the plankton into their mouths through fringes of tough skin, called baleen.

Baleen

Deep water

It is cold and dark in the deepest parts of the ocean. Some animals living there have unusual ways of finding food. A deep-sea angler fish can light up the lure on its head (see below). Smaller animals swim towards the light and the angler fish catches them in its mouth.

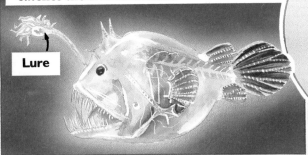

Lure

Exploring underwater

There are still many discoveries to be made about life in the ocean. Scientists use underwater ships, called submersibles, to explore the deepest parts.

Submersible

55

Sea shores and coral reefs

Not all saltwater plants and animals live in the deep oceans. Many live on shores beside the sea, or in shallow water habitats, such as coral reefs. Plants and animals living on shores have to survive in a habitat that changes with the tides. They are under water when the tide is in. When it is out, they are in the open air.

Sandy shores

There are few hiding places on sandy shores. Small animals have to protect themselves so they do not get eaten.

Shrimps have a hard covering and can burrow into the sand.

Turtles live in warm seas. They only come on to the shore to lay their eggs on sandy beaches. Many kinds of turtles are in danger of dying out.

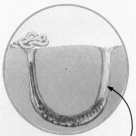

Lugworms spend all their lives buried in the sand, in burrows.

Razorshells have a soft body and two long shells, joined along one side. Two muscles hold these shells closed if the razorshell is in danger.

BEACH ALARM
Many beaches are no longer safe for people or wildlife. They have been spoiled by pollution washed up from the sea, and by people dumping litter on them (see page 60).

Rocky shores

Animals living on rocky shores have plenty of hiding places. Many live in rock pools (pools left behind when the tide goes out).

Shore crabs have a hard shell, called a carapace. They shelter under rocks.

Limpets cling to rocks with a suction foot under their shells. This stops them from being swept away by the tide.

Seaweeds grow in shallow water. They cling to rocks, so they do not get washed away.

Sea anemones use their tentacles to catch shrimps and small fish.

Rock pool

Rock gobies hide in gaps between rocks.

Sea birds

Many birds feed on shores. They make their nests on cliffs, or on the beach.

Puffins catch fish while swimming. They have wide beaks, so they can hold many fish at once.

Oystercatchers use their beaks to dig for shellfish, such as cockles.

Seagulls will eat almost anything. They even search for food on rubbish dumps.

Arctic terns dive into the water to catch fish. They can fly further than any other birds.

Coral reefs

Coral reefs are found in clear, shallow, warm seas. All kinds of colourful and unusual creatures live there. The reefs are made up of the shells of small animals, called coral polyps. As old polyps die, new ones grow on top of their empty shells.

Dead coral

Living polyps

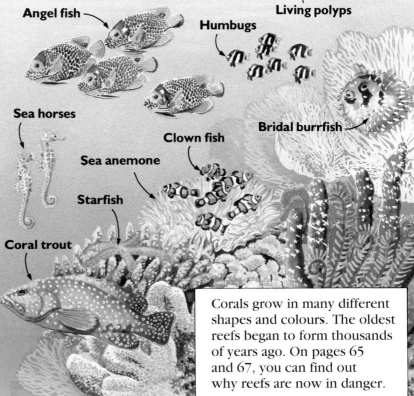

Angel fish

Humbugs

Bridal burrfish

Sea horses

Clown fish

Sea anemone

Starfish

Coral trout

Corals grow in many different shapes and colours. The oldest reefs began to form thousands of years ago. On pages 65 and 67, you can find out why reefs are now in danger.

Australia

The Great Barrier Reef is so large, it can even be seen from space.

The Great Barrier Reef

The Great Barrier Reef in Australia is over 2,000km (1,240 miles) long. It is the largest coral reef in the world. Over 2,000 different kinds of fish live there.

Pollution

On the next four pages, you can find out how water becomes polluted, and how this harms living things. You can also find out what has been done and what can be done to stop pollution and protect wildlife.

Factory waste

For many years, factories have been dumping huge amounts of waste into rivers and seas. This seemed to be a cheap and easy way of getting rid of it. People thought the waste would disappear. In fact, much of it stays in the water for a long time, and is a danger to humans and wildlife.

Waste pouring into rivers often contains harmful chemicals.

Some dangerous waste is dumped at the bottom of the sea.

Some waste is burned out at sea, in large ships. The ash is then dumped in the water.

Belugas in trouble

Beluga whales live in the St Lawrence river, in Canada. This is one of the most polluted rivers in the world. Factories on its banks dump waste into the water. Many belugas have been poisoned.

Beluga whales are also called white whales.

In 1900, there were 5,000 belugas living in this river. Now there are less than 500.

Poisonous PCBs

PCBs are poisonous chemicals. When they are dumped in water, they are taken in by tiny plants and animals. When these are eaten by larger animals, the PCBs are taken in too. Animals, such as whales, at the top of the food chain, may eat many smaller poisoned ones. They then contain dangerous amounts of PCBs.

Factories use PCBs to cool machinery. PCBs have been banned in many countries but are still used in some places.

Dying seals

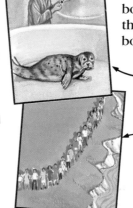

In 1988, over 18,000 common seals in the North Sea died of a disease. Most had PCBs in their bodies. Scientists have found that animals with PCBs in their bodies catch diseases easily.

People saved some seals by giving them injections against the disease.

In Germany, 30,000 people formed a human chain 40km (25 miles) long, across the island of Sylt, to protest against this pollution.

Pollution of groundwater

We cannot see groundwater, so it is hard to know when it has been polluted. Groundwater that is being polluted today may be used as drinking water in many years' time. Here are some of the ways this pollution can happen.

Waste from homes and factories is buried in large pits, called landfills.

Farmers spray their crops with chemicals, called pesticides, to kill insect pests.

All these chemicals may seep through soil into groundwater, and pollute it.

Chemicals, and liquid from rotting waste can leak out and seep into groundwater.

Chemical fertilizers are put on fields to help crops grow.

Pollution facts

★ 20 billion tonnes (22 billion tons) of pollution are dumped into the oceans every year.

★ Sweden has 85,000 lakes. Over 21,000 of these, and about 100,000km (62,000 miles) of its streams and rivers have been polluted by acid rain (see right).

★ There are 400,000 landfills containing dangerous waste in the USA. 10,000 of these need to be made safer immediately.

Acid rain

When fuels, such as oil or coal, are burned in cars or factories, the waste gases mix with the water in air to make acid rain. North America and parts of Europe suffer most from acid rain.

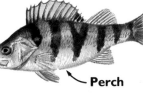

Perch

When acid rain falls on lakes and rivers, it pollutes the water. Then many fish, such as perch and salmon, die.

Animals, such as otters, depend on fish for food. If there are no fish in a lake or river, the otters living there will starve.

59

More pollution

Not all pollution comes from factories or farms. Here are some other ways water becomes polluted.

Dirty beaches

Large amounts of human waste, or sewage, from toilets and drains, are dumped in the sea, often close to the shore. Sewage can be treated to make it safe, but many countries do not do this. Untreated sewage can cause all kinds of diseases.

DANGER! NO SWIMMING

Sewage washes up on to beaches, making them unsafe for swimming.

Making a living

Many people depend on the sea for food. In south-east Asia, one quarter of the people who live near the sea make a living from fishing. Their waters are some of the most polluted by sewage.

Shellfish take in a lot of pollution. In many places, they are no longer safe to eat.

Lobsters
Mussels
Crabs

Dumping rubbish

People dump all kinds of everyday rubbish on beaches and wetlands, or in rivers and ponds. Much of this can be dangerous.

Broken glass and the sharp edges of tin cans can cut people and animals.

Animals, such as turtles, can mistake plastic for food. It stays in their stomachs, making them feel full. They then stop eating, and can starve.

Oil pollution

When oil spills into the sea, it forms a large pool, called a slick, on the surface of the water. The slick can drift to shore, polluting beaches and killing wildlife. In 1991, during the Gulf War, up to two million barrels of oil leaked into the Persian Gulf, from oil wells in Kuwait.

Thousands of sea birds died because oil clogged their feathers, and they could no longer keep warm.

People saved some birds by washing the oil from their feathers.

Dugongs are rare animals that feed on seagrass. They could not eat seagrass covered in oil.

Whales may swallow plastic bags or balloons, thinking they are jellyfish.

Plastic rings that hold cans together can strangle birds, fish and other animals.

Time to stop polluting

Here are some of the ways people have tried to stop pollution. There are many things you can do to help (see pages 70-71). Everybody must work together to keep water clean and safe for people, plants and animals.

Saving Lake Baikal

◀ Lake Baikal is the oldest and deepest lake in the world. It is now being polluted by factories and farms around its shores. Local people are trying to protect the lake and its wildlife from pollution.

Many of Lake Baikal's animals are not found anywhere else.

This poster at a local bus station tells people about the problem. The message says "Save Lake Baikal".

Thirty per cent club

In 1985, 21 countries signed an agreement to try to stop acid rain. They plan to cut down the amount of poisonous gases from factories and power stations by almost one-third (thirty per cent) by 1993.

Rhine Action Plan

In 1980, four countries made the Rhine Action Plan, to try to clean up the River Rhine (see page 51). Factories must change the way they work, so that they make less waste.

Clean-up time

Earlier this century, the River Thames in London, England, was so polluted that no fish could live in it. In 1953, people began treating sewage before putting it into the river. Now 112 kinds of fish live there.

Radioactive waste

Radioactive waste, from nuclear power stations, can be very dangerous. It can change the way living things grow, and may cause cancer. Some radioactive waste stays harmful for thousands of years.

No more dumping

Some radioactive waste used to be sealed in barrels and dumped in the oceans. Then people realised that, one day, the barrels might break up, and the waste would escape. In 1983, all the world's countries agreed to ban the dumping of radioactive waste at sea.

Members of Greenpeace (see page 68) sailed near the dumping ships, to try to stop them from dropping the barrels. This helped many people to find out about the dangers.

Dangers from fishing

People have been fishing since the earliest times. Many still depend on fish for food, and to make a living. Today, fishermen can catch huge amounts of fish. On these pages, you can find out why this is not always a good thing.

Overfishing

If fishermen catch too many of one type of fish, that type can be in danger of dying out. This is called overfishing. When it happens, fishermen suffer as well, because they can no longer make a living.

In 1976, there were so few herrings left in the North Sea that herring fishing was banned for 7 years to allow numbers to increase.

In Lake Victoria, in Africa, some tilapias are in danger from overfishing.

Overfishing does not happen when people agree to limit the number of fish they catch.

Modern fishing boats

Modern fishing boats can catch up to 200 tonnes (220 tons) of fish at one time. Their large nets have small holes, so the fish cannot escape.

Trawl net

Catching krill

In the Southern Ocean, there are huge numbers of small animals called krill. They are an important part of the food chain there. Over the last ten years, some countries have started catching large amounts of krill. We must be careful not to overfish krill, as many other animals depend on them for food.

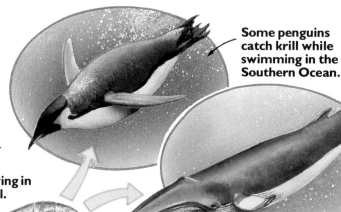

Some penguins catch krill while swimming in the Southern Ocean.

Crabeater seals living in Antarctica eat krill.

Krill are small shrimps.

Krill are the main food for baleen whales, such as minke whales.

In 1982, 35 countries made an agreement to try to protect krill from overfishing.

Dolphins and tuna

In the Eastern Pacific, dolphins and yellowfin tuna swim together. Dolphins swim near the surface and tuna swim a little way below.

When fishermen see dolphins, they know tuna may also be there. They put out nets to catch the tuna but many dolphins are caught too.

If nets had bigger holes, young fish could escape. They could then grow and breed, stopping numbers from getting too low.

The top of the net is on the surface of the water.

Purse-seine net

Dolphins and tuna swim into the net through the back.

When this rope is pulled from above, the two sides come together and the net closes.

Dolphins drown if they cannot reach the surface to breathe.

Some fishermen lower the net before pulling it in, so dolphins can swim out over the top.

Caught by mistake

Huge fishing nets, called drift-nets, which can be up to 56km (35 miles) long, are used in deep oceans. They are made of thin nylon, which is almost invisible in the water. All kinds of animals get trapped in them. Since 1991, drift-nets have been banned in the South Pacific.

Kemp's ridley turtles have almost died out, because so many have drowned in shrimp nets in the Gulf of Mexico.

Sea birds, such as albatrosses, dive into the water for fish, and get their feet or wings caught in nets.

Yellowfin tuna are a type of large fish.

Lost or torn nets of all types float through the oceans and carry on trapping animals, such as seals and small whales.

In the past 30 years, over five million dolphins have been killed in tuna nets – about one every three minutes. Many people think there should be a law protecting dolphins from being killed in this way. On page 71, you can find out how you can help to save them.

63

Hunting and collecting

People have always hunted water animals for their shells, skins, fur or meat. When too many of one type, or species, of animal are killed, that species can die out, or become extinct. Many species have already been hunted to extinction. Hundreds more are now in danger.

Beavers

100 years ago, North American beavers almost became extinct. They had been hunted so that their fur could be used to make hats. Laws were made to protect beavers, which saved them from extinction, but over half a million are still killed each year.

Baby beavers cannot survive if their mother is killed.

Whale hunting

Hundreds of years ago, people began hunting whales for their meat, and to make oil from their fat. First, slow swimmers, such as right whales, were hunted. Then, with faster boats, other whales could be caught too. Today, many species are in danger. On page 69, you can find out what people are doing to save whales.

Before hunting started, there were 100,000 right whales. Today, there are only about 3,000.

Turtles in trouble

Turtles are hunted for their meat and shells. Their eggs are dug up to be sold for food. All sea turtles, and some freshwater turtles, are now in danger of extinction.

Turtle shells are used to make jewellery and combs. Plastic copies look the same, but do not harm turtles.

Hawksbill, ridley and green turtles are all killed for their shells.

Hawksbill turtle

In Malaysia, people have set up a project to help leatherback turtles. Some of their eggs are dug up from the beach and taken to a safe place, called a sanctuary. When the baby turtles hatch, they are taken back to the same beach, and set free. ▶

Baby seals

In Canada, thousands of baby harp seals used to be killed every year, so that their fur could be made into coats. Many people thought this was cruel, and began to protest against it. There is now a law against killing these baby seals, but many older harp seals are still being killed.

Crocodiles

In 1950, there were large numbers of crocodiles in some parts of the world. Then people started buying shoes, bags and belts made from their skins. Most species are now very rare because of this.

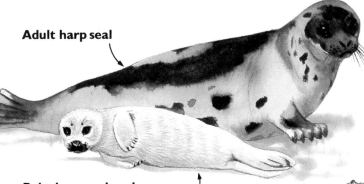

Adult harp seal

Gharials are river crocodiles which live in northern India. By 1974, there were fewer than 200 left. People are now trying to save gharials by hatching their eggs in sanctuaries.

Baby harp seals only keep their beautiful, white coats for the first 15 days of their lives.

Gharial

Dangers from collecting

Some people collect unusual fish and keep them in tanks. Corals and shells are also collected, and made into jewellery or ornaments. These are sold to tourists, or to other countries. Many species are rare because of this.

In the Caribbean Sea, black coral is almost extinct, because so much has been made into jewellery.

Some sea animals are collected so that their beautiful shells can be made into lamps or ornaments.

Oysters and freshwater mussels are collected for the pearls inside their shells. Pearls are used to make jewellery, such as necklaces.

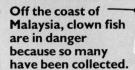

Off the coast of Malaysia, clown fish are in danger because so many have been collected.

Changing habitats

The main reason that so many species are becoming extinct is that their habitats are being destroyed or disturbed by people.

Each species of plant or animal is suited to its living place. If this habitat changes, the species may not survive.

Habitat destruction

People destroy water habitats so they can make use of the land. Here are some of the ways this happens.

Rivers, ponds and wetlands are drained, and filled in with stones and soil to make the ground level.

Houses, shops and factories can be built on this new land.

Before | After

Farmers cut down trees, and other plants, from riverbanks, so that they have more room for fields.

Here are some of the plants and animals which are in danger because their habitats have been destroyed.

Storks lose their feeding places when wetlands are destroyed.

Lotuses in Egypt and southern marsh orchids in Britain are in danger because their marsh homes have been drained.

Lotus

Marsh orchid

Frogs and toads have nowhere to lay their eggs when their breeding ponds are filled in.

Toads on roads

Toads return to the same pond or lake each year, to lay their eggs. When busy roads are built along their routes, many toads are run over.

On some roads, there are signs warning drivers to look out for toads crossing.

Protected areas

Protected areas are places that have been set aside where plants and animals can live safely. People can go to most of them, but activities, such as fishing and building, are controlled, so as not to disturb wildlife. Protected sea areas are called marine reserves.

Threats from tourists

With modern transport, people can travel all over the world. Places that used to be quiet wildlife habitats are now popular holiday areas. Animals often suffer when this happens.

Baby turtles

Moonlight on the water helps baby turtles know which way to go to get to the sea. Bright lights from roads and buildings near the beach confuse them so that they set off in the wrong direction.

Monk seals

When tourists started going to beaches around the Mediterranean Sea, the monk seals living there were scared away. Today, there are only about 500 Mediterranean monk seals left.

Coral reefs

Coral reefs are easily harmed. Tourists can damage a reef with their feet, while swimming nearby. In south-east Asia, coral is dug up and used to make buildings, such as airports.

Hotels, shops and roads are built for tourists to use. Many habitats are destroyed to make room for these.

Wild animals are very nervous. They will not come near a beach if there are people sitting or playing on it.

Motor boats make a lot of noise and their propellers can harm, or even kill, animals such as dolphins and seals.

Thousands of sea birds, such as frigatebirds, lay their eggs on Aldabra Atoll, a marine reserve in the Seychelles, in the Indian Ocean.

All kinds of unusual wildlife, such as greater flamingoes, live in the Camargue, a protected wetland area in southern France.

Many more of these safe areas in or near water are needed, if we are going to protect habitats successfully.

67

Working towards a safer world

Many people are now trying to protect water habitats and the wildlife living there, so that plants and animals can live in a safer world. Below, you can find out about how they are doing this, and about some of the species that have been protected.

Conservation groups

There are many groups working to protect water. They tell people about the dangers and set up projects to save species. Some try to get laws passed to stop hunting, pollution and so on.

Groups, such as Greenpeace and Friends of the Earth, often carry out unusual actions, to draw people's attention to problems, and to raise money.

Friends of the Earth has a globe as its symbol.

← These members of Greenpeace hung on ropes from a bridge over the River Rhine, to protest against pollution.

Seal success

In 1900, there were fewer than 100 northern elephant seals left, because of hunting. In 1972, a law was passed in the USA, making it illegal to kill these seals. Today, thousands breed every year at the Año Nuevo State Reserve, a wildlife park in California, USA.

← Elephant seals are the largest seal species.

Peace for Antarctica

In 1959, 16 countries signed the Antarctic Treaty, to try to protect Antarctica from pollution and disturbance. One of the things they had to decide was whether to allow mining. In 1991, they agreed that no mining was to be allowed in Antarctica for at least 50 years.

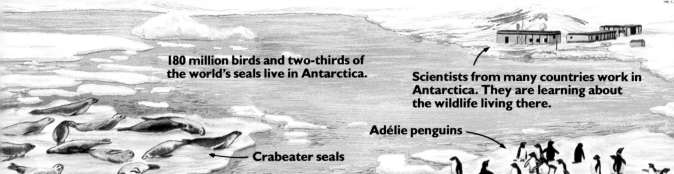

180 million birds and two-thirds of the world's seals live in Antarctica.

Scientists from many countries work in Antarctica. They are learning about the wildlife living there.

Adélie penguins

Crabeater seals

Protected pelicans

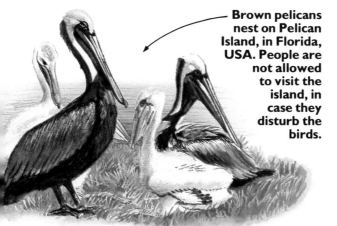

Brown pelicans nest on Pelican Island, in Florida, USA. People are not allowed to visit the island, in case they disturb the birds.

In the 1960s, brown pelicans in the USA were in danger because they were eating fish that had been poisoned by pesticides. In 1972, these pesticides were banned. Since then, the number of pelicans has greatly increased.

Saving whales

By the 1970s, many species of whales were in great danger because of hunting. In 1986, 36 countries agreed to ban the hunting of larger whales. Every year, they meet to decide whether to continue this ban. They also have to decide whether smaller whales need protection too.

People hope the ban will help to save whales, such as humpbacks, from becoming extinct.

Laws and agreements

★ In Florida, USA, local people have made laws to keep beach lighting low at turtle-nesting times (see page 67).

★ In the Seychelles, anyone who kills or harms a sea mammal can be sent to prison for up to five years.

★ Since 1988, 31 countries have agreed to ban their ships from dumping plastic rubbish into the sea.

★ In 1976, 18 countries signed the Mediterranean Action Plan, to try to clean up the Mediterranean Sea, one of the most polluted in the world.

Balicasag Island

In 1985, a marine reserve was set up on Balicasag Island, in the Philippines. Local people took part in starting up the reserve and now help to run it.

They put up information signs and tell tourists about the area. They are also learning ways of making a living which do not harm wildlife.

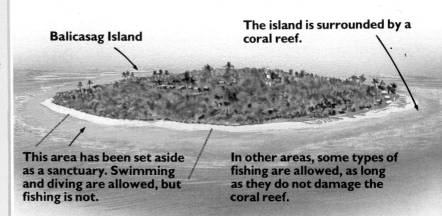

Balicasag Island

The island is surrounded by a coral reef.

This area has been set aside as a sanctuary. Swimming and diving are allowed, but fishing is not.

In other areas, some types of fishing are allowed, as long as they do not damage the coral reef.

What you can do

There are many things we can all do to protect the world's water. Here are some ideas. Everyone can do something to help.

Make less waste

All the rubbish from homes, schools and offices has to be put somewhere. A lot is buried underground and this can pollute groundwater (see page 59). You can help to reduce this pollution by making less waste.

Save paper by writing on both sides of every sheet.

Used batteries leak harmful chemicals. Try using rechargeable ones instead. They contain chemicals too, but can be re-used many times.

Plastic containers, such as ice-cream tubs, can be re-used for storing things.

Many of the things we buy are packaged in layers of paper and plastic. Try to buy things which have less packaging.

Fast-food restaurants often use a lot of packaging, which is thrown away almost immediately.

Before you throw something away, make sure that you really cannot use it any more.

Recycling

Glass, metal and most kinds of paper can be recycled (turned back into new glass, metal or paper). You could collect used bottles, cans and paper at home and at school. Your local authority or conservation group will have information about recycling in your area.

Look out for this symbol on things such as paper and cans. It means that they can be recycled.

In many towns, there are special bins where you can put glass bottles, cans or newspapers to be recycled.

Saving water

The less water you use, the less dirty water goes down the drain. This means there is less sewage to be poured into rivers and seas. Here are some ways to save water.

- **Try not to leave the water running while you brush your teeth. Only turn it on to rinse your brush.**
- **If you can, have showers instead of baths. They use about half as much water.**
- **Ask an adult to mend dripping taps. One leaking tap could fill 52 baths in a year.**

Balloons and bags

If balloons and plastic bags end up in the sea, they can harm water animals (see page 60). You can help in the following ways.

Try not to let go of balloons when you are outdoors. The wind may carry them to the sea.

Re-use plastic bags as much as possible or, even better, go shopping with a canvas bag or basket instead.

Dolphin-friendly tuna

You can now buy cans of tuna fish which are labelled to say that dolphins were not harmed when the tuna was caught.

Look for labels like this.

If your local shops do not sell dolphin-friendly tuna, ask them why. Tell them you will only buy this kind of tuna.

DOLPHIN FRIENDLY

Safer waste

You can also help to protect water and the wildlife living there by making some kinds of waste safer before throwing them away, or washing them down the drain.

Cut up the plastic rings that hold cans together before you put them in the bin. Then they cannot harm animals (see page 60).

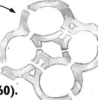

Some cleaning products have harmful chemicals in them. Waste water containing these chemicals can end up in the sea. Try to get your family to buy safer products.

Litter

Litter dropped on a beach, near a river or from a boat can harm water animals. Always put litter in a bin, or take it home instead. Even if you are not near water, litter can be carried a long way by the wind. Every bit makes a difference.

Taking action

Local conservation groups often get together to clean up beaches, or areas near rivers, ponds and lakes. There are some groups especially for children. Your local library should have information about groups in your area.

SAVE OUR STREAM

Always make sure there is an adult with you when you go near water.

Facts and records

Whales and dolphins

★Blue whales are bigger than the largest dinosaurs that ever lived. They can make sounds louder than a jet plane.

★Dolphins can swim at speeds of over 56km(35 miles) per hour.

★The brain of a sperm whale is the largest of any animal on Earth. It is about 8 times the size of a human brain.

Coral facts

★A third of all the species of fish in the world live in coral reefs.

★Coral grows very slowly. Some of the most common species grow less than 8cm(3in) a year.

★The Great Barrier Reef (see page 57) covers a larger area than the whole of the UK.

Net amounts

★If all the nets used by Japan to catch squid in the Pacific Ocean were put together, they would stretch to the moon 3 times.

★In the Pacific Ocean, about 800 boats put out 50,000km(31,000 miles) of drift-nets each night – enough to go around the Earth one and a quarter times.

Oldest lake

★Lake Baikal (see page 61), the world's oldest lake, is 20-25 million years old. The second oldest is Lake Tanganyika, in Central Africa, which is 2 million years old.

Amazing Antarctica

★Antarctica covers a tenth of the world's surface. It is larger than Australia and more than half the size of the USSR.

★Nine-tenths of the world's ice and seven-tenths of its fresh water are in Antarctica.

★Antarctica is the coldest place on Earth. The temperature can fall as low as $-88°C(-126°F)$, the ice can be up to 3km(2 miles) deep and the wind can blow at 322km(200 miles) per hour.

Loads of rubbish

★10 billion aluminium* cans are used in Britain every year – enough to reach to the moon and back, laid end to end.

★A third of all the rubbish on rubbish dumps is packaging.

★Up to a million sea creatures are killed every year by plastic bags and other plastic rubbish thrown into the sea.

Deepest ocean

★The deepest part of any ocean is the Mariana Trench in the Pacific Ocean. It is 10,924m(35,839ft) deep. If you put Mount Everest (the tallest mountain) into the Mariana Trench, you would not be able to see its top.

Longest river

★The longest river in the world is the River Nile which is 6,670km (4,145 miles) long. It starts in Burundi, in Central Africa, and flows to Egypt, where it comes out into the Mediterranean Sea.

*aluminum (US)

Index

Printed in Belgium